'No more exams. No m[...]
blissful weeks painting in the country – then, art college
at last. Just paint, paint, paint!'

This is Cathy Harlow's vision of the future, but one that
is cruelly shattered when she meets Paul Devlin, the lead
guitarist with the rock group Easy Connection and a
millionaire superstar. She didn't realize she was trespassing on his land and the punishment he exacts is a harsh
one.

College subsequently becomes more of a nightmare
than a dream, even with the help of kind, reliable Nick,
as Dev pursues her relentlessly and Cathy finds herself
powerless to resist!

A powerful and unusual love story set against the
manipulative world of rock music and the colourful world
of art.

# Easy Connections

## LIZ BERRY

PUFFIN BOOKS

Puffin Books, Penguin Books Ltd, Harmondsworth, Middlesex, England
Viking Penguin Inc., 40 West 23rd Street, New York, New York 10010, U.S.A.
Penguin Books Australia Ltd, Ringwood, Victoria, Australia
Penguin Books Canada Ltd, 2801 John Street, Markham, Ontario, Canada L3R 1B4
Penguin Books (N.Z.) Ltd, 182–190 Wairau Road, Auckland 10, New Zealand

—

First published by Victor Gollancz Ltd 1983
Published in Puffin Books 1984

—

—

Printed and bound in Great Britain by
Cox & Wyman Ltd, Reading
Filmset in Monophoto Photina by
Northumberland Press Ltd, Gateshead

# *Author's note*

Except for the famous bands mentioned briefly by name in the text, all incidents and characters in this story, including the bands Easy Connection and Night Mission, are entirely invented and imaginary.

# One

The sky was apricot gold and the September shadows lengthened across the grass. At the edge of the field by the stream, Cathy continued to paint, unaware of the time passing or of the semi-circle of young cows behind her.

It was only when one of the cows snorted close to her ear that she looked round and found the ring of moony eyes gazing at her. Giggling, she clapped her hands and shooed the cows away. Where had they come from? They hadn't been there when she started painting nearly three hours ago. Could they really be watching her paint?

Smiling, she went back to the painting on the easel. Yesterday she had made two pencil studies of the plants and trees, and today she had brought oils and a canvas to try to capture the purple brown of the tree and the weeds, dark in the water of the stream. Now the painting was almost finished and she was reasonably content with her afternoon's work. Mr Arnold, at any rate, would like it.

She remembered then, feeling strange, that Mr Arnold wouldn't see it. School was over for ever.

The cows had retreated only a few steps, and soon they were back, close together, snorting and inching forward. She waved her arms to make them go away, but they looked so shy and wistful, like the boys at the end-of-term disco, that she threw back her head and laughed aloud.

Frightened by the unexpected noise, the cows lifted their heads, their eyes showing white. They turned about, jostling each other, and lumbered off up the field. The last one got a stray kick and galloped away panicking. Its tail, swinging wildly, caught one thin leg of her easel.

The easel toppled backwards. The painting, fixed insecurely, sailed over the top, made a leisurely somersault, and landed, smack, face up in the nearby stream. It began to float gaily downstream.

Cathy began to laugh helplessly. She kicked off her sandals and waded into midstream. The painting moved forward, just out of reach. She grabbed at it, unsuccessfully, and it floated forward another metre. She tried to move more quickly, stumbled, her feet slipping on the mossy pebbles, lost her balance and fell forward with a splash into the water.

She pulled herself up, soaked, and sat down on the largest stepping stone in the middle of the stream, hysterical with laughter. Monty Python, she thought. Buster Keaton!

When she managed to get a grip of her hilarity, she saw that the painting had now lodged itself securely between two boulders. She waded downstream, still laughing, picked it up, and shook the water from it. She made her way to the bank and propped the painting against a bush to let the hot sun dry out the canvas. The oily surface seemed none the worse for its dipping, not even scratched, but she thought the stretchers would probably warp. The canvas would need restretching. And the sun was too hot.

In the end she put the painting against a tree trunk shadowed by a bush so that it would dry out more slowly. The final details could be done at the house later.

She began to clean her palette and brushes and packed them away with the easel and paints into her old straw bag. She threw away the turps under a bush, wiped out the tin and put it into the bag. Finally she rubbed her hands on a rag, sniffing at them appreciatively. There was something about the smell of turpentine. Her hands were small, with thin fingers. They moved swiftly and deftly. Tomorrow she would start a painting of the greenhouses at the market garden.

Her chores finished, she became aware again of the water dribbling unpleasantly down her back. She took off her teeshirt, wrung it out and, hesitating, draped it over a bush to dry. She would have liked to take off her velour shorts too, which were clinging uncomfortably, but the cows had given her an odd feeling of being watched, even though they were at the far end of the field now.

Her hair, which had been neatly tied back, was curling in damp tendrils round her forehead and shoulders. She shook it back and sat down in a patch of sunlight to dry it, leaning back on her arms.

The sun was warm on her body. She closed her eyes, feeling deeply peaceful and happy.

No more exams. No more boring holiday work in the packing factory. Just two more blissful weeks painting here in the country – then, art college at last! On her own, in her own bedsit. *Free*. No more hassles with Aunt Cass about the light on at two o'clock in the morning. Just paint, paint, paint!

She wondered how Aunt Cass was getting on in Edinburgh. After fifty years in London she had decided to go back to her old home. Cathy thought, suddenly, that she would miss crusty old Aunt Cass, who wasn't a real aunt at all, just the lady who had lived next door. But when her mother had died suddenly two years ago, Aunt Cass had offered to look after her during term time, so that she could finish her exams without changing schools. There was no one else. Her father had disappeared to Australia years before and her only brother lived out in Nethercombe with his wife and baby son. She stayed with them during the holidays.

Cathy had taken her A-level Art with distinction, when she was only sixteen, and the last year she had spent a lot of time at the local polytechnic, following (unofficially, because she was too young) the art foundation course, and getting extra A-levels. She was sure that this was the reason they had offered her a place at the London College of Art, a year earlier than usual, plus, of course, her folder of work and the recommendations of her teachers. Her special home circumstances had counted too. She was very lucky. It was almost unheard of to get into College before you were actually eighteen. She might have had to wait another whole year! It seemed too good to be true.

She smiled and stretched out luxuriously. It was nearly time for the evening meal. Another few minutes and she would find her sandals ...

The young man on the higher, opposite bank of the stream, half-hidden by the trees, was enchanted.

He had been watching her for over half an hour now. He had seen the ring of animals round the oblivious girl, and he had stayed to see what happened. He had enjoyed the knock-about comedy act in the stream. Her laughter had delighted him – and he had not met many girls who would laugh in that kind of situation – and he had even enjoyed watching her pack. The striptease was a surprise bonus.

He was so absorbed that he did not hear his friend come up behind him.

'What are you looking at?'

'You nearly gave me a heart attack.' He got up, grinning and flipped his fingers. 'Nice.'

They stood, staring across at the girl lying in the sunlit meadow. She was about seventeen, delicate and slender, but with full breasts, her skin a clear creamy rose. Her hair, dishevelled, shone golden in the sun. She was barefoot, and there was a cut on her shin.

His friend stared blankly, taking in the state of the girl, then weary disgust swept across his face. He swore explosively.

'Not already! How did this one get in?'

The other began to laugh. 'Listen . . .' But his friend was already striding and scrambling down the bank under the overhanging trees.

'Hey, *you*!'

Cathy heard the laughter and the crackling twigs. She had been nearly asleep, but she sat up hastily, trying to focus through the red haze the sun had printed on her eyelids.

'Hey, you girl!'

The furious voice got through her daze and her vision cleared miraculously.

Two young men were standing a few metres away, on the other side of the stream.

Cathy blinked, rubbed her eyes and stared again. They were still there, staring back at her, silent now. They stood shoulder to shoulder, just above average height, very straight and graceful. They were strangely alike. Lithe, slim-hipped. They were both fair, but one was ash-blond with short, rough-cut hair, and the other had long, shoulder-length curly hair, dark gold. But it was their faces that made Cathy take an extra deep breath. They were beautiful.

She thought, confused, that you couldn't call men beautiful. Handsome. But the two faces that looked at her silently and intently across the stream were *beautiful*. Coldly beautiful, with perfect bone structure, slightly tilted eyes, clear tanned skin and wide, clear-cut, full mouths. For a crazy moment she thought they must have walked out of the deeper woods behind. Tolkien. Elvish Lords! Then the one with the long hair spoke, and her reason righted itself. He was very angry.

'What you doing here, girl?'

She blushed vividly and folded her arms around her. She was angry with herself for being found like this, annoyed by his unnecessary rudeness. She caught his faint American accent. She was doing no harm. What right had he to shout at her?

'Ramble on, boy!'

It was a fair imitation, and his friend gave way to a new burst of laughter.

'You too!' She got up, hoping they could not see the way her knees were trembling, and went over to the bush. She turned her back and pulled on her wet teeshirt.

The long-haired one, even more furious now at the mockery, groped for his English accent which had got overlaid in his four months in the States.

'You're trespassing on my land!'

'This is Cox's Farm.'

'*My* farm!'

Cathy's dark, grey-violet eyes looked him over carefully, taking in the long fingers, the tight jeans, the flowery silk shirt, unbuttoned with a kind of careless elegance, to reveal a bare chest and a strangely carved stone pendant. He was not embarrassed by her scrutiny.

'You don't look like a farmer to me.'

Another splutter of laughter from the short-haired one, who was wearing jeans and a leather jacket, and a copper disc on a thick chain.

'You know damn well who we are, or you wouldn't be lying around like that, just waiting to be found!'

'I was painting!'

'God, they think of everything!' he said to his friend. 'I don't see any painting, paints, easel ...'

'They're in the bag, there. I've just packed up.'

'Anyone can borrow the gear. Where's the painting? Do you

generally paint like – that?' He flipped his hand towards the wet shirt. She eased it away from her skin, blushing furiously.

'Of course not! I was painting and these cows came along and pushed my painting in the stream and I went to get it and fell in.'

It sounded unlikely, and the humour of the situation got to her again, and she bit her lip to stop laughing. His eyes darkened dangerously.

'Bullocks,' said the short-haired one, gently. 'They're bullocks, love.'

She stared at him, diverted. 'What! Are you *sure*? How do you know ...?' She stopped dead, but it was too late.

He raised an eyebrow, his eyes gleaming. 'You want a demonstration?'

Cathy, scarlet, could not help laughing. 'I never noticed.'

'As the actress said to the bishop. I bet the boys just love you.' They both laughed.

'That does it!' said the long-haired one, losing his temper completely and striding across the stream on the large flat stepping stones.

'You're coming back to the house with me, and we'll see what the fuzz have to say. I've had enough.' He seized her bag, and clamping a hand on her shoulder propelled her, roughly, across the stream and up the bank, slipping and stumbling. He was surprisingly strong.

'Oh, please!' she said, trying to twist away. 'Won't you *please* let me explain? I don't know who you think I am or what I want, but please don't call the police. Honestly, it's not necessary. Please, please wait.'

'Yes, I thought you wouldn't find that so funny!'

'But if you saw the cows, I mean, bullocks, you must have seen me painting.'

'I didn't see any bullocks. All I saw was *you*, lying down, without your shirt!'

'Listen,' said the short-haired one, trying to restrain his laughter. 'It's true, honestly. There were bullocks. I can vouch for them. And she did fall in the stream.'

His friend shot him a glinting, sidelong glance.

'I guess I thought you'd say something like that, Chris, ol' buddy. You saw it all, I suppose.'

'Nearly all.' He laughed. 'I was hoping.'

'I came along too soon?'

'Maybe.' He winked irrepressibly at Cathy. 'Dev thinks it's all a cock and bull story.'

Cathy bit her lip again, but she was too scared to laugh aloud.

They went across the field towards the farm. Dev kept his hand on her shoulder, the strong fingers biting into her bones. The one called Chris walked on the other side of her, still laughing, trying to confirm her story. She looked at them sideways, not understanding their jokey, allusive conversation, only knowing that Dev did not believe Chris either.

What was the matter with him? Why was his temper so trigger happy? She hadn't *done* anything. Now she was so close she could feel the tension in his body, and saw that there was a kind of edgy desperation about him which frightened her. She walked as close as she could to Chris, but although he joked and laughed, and seemed kinder, she realized that his laughter was coming too quickly, too hectically to be quite natural. She shivered. Had they been taking drugs?

There was no point in trying to get away. It would only make it worse. She would have to let things take their course. Jim would be furious.

She suddenly felt very strange. It was as though she had done this many times before, walked across fields with these two. It was as though she already knew them. Knew them very well indeed. But she was sure she had never seen them. Neither of them was the sort you could possibly forget. She glanced up and met Chris's light grey eyes. His expression was unreadable and he had stopped laughing. She looked hastily at Dev. He was looking at her too. His grey eyes were very dark.

They had crossed the far field, entered a belt of trees and come out on to a gravelled walk. 'Ouch!'

'What's the matter now?'

She said, 'It's the gravel. It's hurting my feet.'

He looked down at her feet, exasperated. They were bleeding in several places from the stones in the stream.

'For Pete's sake, what have you done with your shoes?'

'They're in the water meadow. You dragged me off before I could get them.'

He said grimly, 'We'll go across the lawn.'

She had not seen Cox's Farm for over a year. Then the grass had been overgrown, the windows of the big old Regency house boarded up. It was a long time since it had been a farm. Some of the fields were used by Mr Hubble who farmed the other side of the village.

She was staggered at the changes. The house had been lovingly restored. Its beautiful golden stone had been cleaned; the broken outbuildings had been pulled down. Now everything was glossy and gleaming, the lawns smooth, the flower-beds well kept. The door under the pillared porch was propped open with a shiny brass bell. There was a black Bentley on the raked gravel. Honeysuckle and roses rioted over the stable-yard wall, and through the arch she saw a middle-aged man in a check shirt washing down a large red foreign car with black windows. He grinned when he saw them.

'Nice bit of gingerbread you've found there.'

Chris laughed, but Dev grunted irritably.

There had been a garden the other side of the stable. She said, staring, 'I'm glad you left the old stone barn. It's beautiful.'

Dev looked at her. 'You know the place?'

'What have you done to the knot garden? It was there, the other side of the stable.'

'I wanted a swimming pool,' he said, shortly.

'It was three hundred years old!' She was incredulous. 'You dug up the knot garden to make a swimming pool?'

He shot her a glance of acute dislike. 'You can't swim in a knot garden, sweetheart!'

They came to the edge of the lawn and, hardly stopping in his stride, he picked her up effortlessly and carried her across the gravel, into the stone-paved hall. It was done before she had time to struggle, and she felt how strong and hard his shoulder muscles were under the extraordinary shirt.

'I thought only brides got carried over thresholds,' she said, embarrassed, trying to joke. But his face above her was dark, ruthless, and she was scared stiff now.

She had not really believed that he was the owner, and she was trying hard to remember what she had heard lately about Cox's Farm. Mary had said an army of village women had been sent in to clean it up. Then interior decorators had moved in. Nobody had clapped eyes yet on the new owner. He was out of the country most of the time. There was supposed to be a housekeeping couple looking after the place, but nobody had seen them, either. All the village knew that an immense sum of money must have been spent installing electrically operated gates and repairing the high walls of the estate. There had been a wild rumour, based on this, that the owner was someone important in show biz.

Cathy looked at him intently under her lashes, as he put her down, ungently, in the middle of the hall floor, but she did not recognize him at all.

He went straight to the telephone on a low table near the huge open fire place, and dialled a number without looking it up.

'Dev, are you sure you're doing the right thing?' Chris dropped on to a long, scarlet leather sofa that stood on a scarlet and black Eastern carpet.

'Mind your own business. I've spent fifty thousand making this place private, and I'm not having any damned boilers wandering around.'

Chris looked at her and smiled, ruefully shrugging his shoulders and spreading out his hands. She smiled back, shyly, gratefully, to show there were no hard feelings. He was really very attractive.

She saw then that Dev was looking at her sardonically. She heard the telephone engaged signal. He cursed and dialled again, and went on staring at her.

This time he got through. 'Paul Devlin, Cox's Farm.' Her grey-violet eyes were clear, looking into his and he could have sworn the name meant nothing to her. A good actress too, he thought. 'I've got an intruder. A girl.' His eyes moved over her, slowly, insolently. 'No, not armed. Not dangerous.'

A flush burned her skin deeply, and she had to turn away, swallowing. He smiled, satisfied, confirmed in his suspicions.

'Thanks, I'd appreciate it.'

He put the receiver down, and sat on the sofa next to Chris, stretching out his long legs. 'He's coming along. Sit down.'

'No, thanks.'

He continued to watch her like a cat. 'If you run, I'll smack you!'

She glared at him, but knew he was telling the truth. His temper was too unstable to take a chance.

Chris, slumped on the sofa, his head on the low back, was watching her too. She had no illusions about what she looked like. Her hair looked as though she had just got up, curling into tendrils. Her shorts and shirt were clinging to her embarrassingly, and her legs and arms were muddy with stream water, probably her face too.

Let them look, she thought defiantly. I don't care!

Now they were sitting down they seemed utterly exhausted, not relaxed. There was an unnatural tension about them, and the pressure of their joint, silent gaze was unnerving, almost sinister. She prowled uncomfortably about the room. After today she would not see them again, anyway.

Then, suddenly, it *really* did not matter. She forgot the two strange young men.

Over the fireplace, glowing in scarlet and gold and orange with streaks of livid green, was an oil painting. An original de Stael. Hardly believing, she went over and stood on tiptoe, resting her hands on the elegant white marble. Three musicians playing jazz. The paint was thick, luscious, each wide rough stroke standing for itself, unaltered, oozing at the edges into another stroke. He must have used a putty knife – something like that, she thought. Not a stroke wasted. Essence of jazz. She loved jazz. She loved de Stael. She drew a long, ragged breath. It glowed so much more than the reproductions in books.

In the recess next to the fireplace was another de Stael, smaller, of a seaside place. Five areas of colour, interlocking, and he had everything he needed to show an African beach, with the heat hammering from a vermilion sky. Next to it, on the shadowy return wall, was another oil painting, not de Stael.

It was a dark picture, with a fire burning through, or perhaps glowing coals, and in the coals, a hand. A hand? Holding an object, cool, diaphanous, ice? Diamonds? Dripping cold fire and stars.

Dev was irritated with her utter concentration. It was a new experience for him. Girls were never detached and oblivious when he was around.

'I'm glad you like the paintings.'

His voice came to her, sarcastic, savage. She turned and looked at him, dazed, as though she had forgotten he was there.

'They're beautiful! How did you get hold of a de Stael like that?'

He said, cynically, 'Money buys everything.'

She turned back to the paintings, and his temper leaped. 'You don't have to keep up the pose now, you know. All right, so you can spot a de Stael, but it won't make any difference. The police are on their way.'

She ignored him, looking at the strange painting. 'Who did this other one?'

There was no reply. She turned, surprised, and met the two pairs of eyes, so similar, so different. Then Chris jerked his head sideways at Dev.

'*You* did? You're a painter?'

'Oh, for Chrissake! Drop it!' He sprang to his feet, stalked to the window, moved uncontrollably back to the fireplace, and finally walked out.

She looked uncertainly at Chris. He did not move. She took a step towards the open door.

'No. Don't try it.' His voice was soft, expressionless.

Dev came back with a glass of colourless spirit, and drank it, lounging back on the sofa. She stood in the centre, watching him warily, glancing occasionally at Chris, who looked back, kindly, but neutral.

'It's his house. I visit.'

She shrugged, trying to avoid their eyes.

The room became quiet again, almost eerily motionless, as though they were all suspended in time. The strange tension grew. Cathy could not look away from them now. Their glances touched and locked. We're talking to each other without words, she thought, suddenly panic-stricken, and forced her mind to go blank, because she did not want to understand what they were saying. She must not look at them, *either* of them.

At last, far away at the other side of the park, she thought she heard the sound of a car and began to relax.

At the same moment, down the central broad staircase, came an extremely beautiful girl. She had a perfect oval face, made up to a pale mask. The mouth was a dark purple. The eyes were heavy, dark-rimmed, but when Cathy looked into them, she found they were shockingly dead. The pupils were dilated, and she did not seem to be focusing properly. So it *was* drugs! Cathy shivered involuntarily. Was that the reason for all this money? Were they some sort of international drug-smuggling ring?

The girl was wearing a fabulous, skin-tight, disco outfit, with a bare midriff and a deeply plunging neckline, which revealed her equally fabulous figure. She walked so quietly that she might have been a zombie. Neither Chris nor Dev took any notice of her and Cathy wondered which of them owned her. She sat down, ignoring Cathy, and began to flick through the pages of a magazine.

'*Rock Life* rang earlier. They want a feature interview. I gave them Bill's number.'

Cathy jumped several inches. The girl's voice was cold, metallic, American-accented. And then, suddenly, everything slotted together. The beautiful young men, the fantastic house, the fabulous cars, the wall-to-wall wealth, the paranoia, the drugs.

'Pop stars!' She began to laugh. 'You're pop stars!' Her laughter exploded as her fright dissolved. She coughed to catch her breath and self-control. 'You gave me a fright. I thought you were dope smugglers.' A fresh wave of laughter hit her. 'And *you* think I'm a fan, or one of those girls – what do you call them – who go round after the groups.'

'Groupies.'

'Hookers.'

Neither of them had moved. Their heads back on the sofa, they watched her through half-closed eyes, as though they were posing for a photograph. Chris was smiling, but Dev's eyes had gone absolutely black and glittering.

'And, oh dear . . .' She went off into laughter again, remembering his absolute certainty that she knew who he was. 'I didn't mean to offend you. I'm so sorry I don't recognize you or your names.'

She breathed deeply trying to regain control. 'Y-you see pop isn't my thing. I don't know anything about it. I don't listen to it. Don't know the names of the pop stars or anything.'

'Rock,' said Dev, savagely.

'Rock then, whatever you call it. I don't know anything about it. Well, I might know the current Number One, but that's all.'

'What *is* your bag, sweetie?' Chris sat up suddenly and lit a cigarette, looking more human and natural. He was grinning at her. She smiled back. 'Jazz, folk, some classical. Mainly jazz at the moment.'

'Who?'

'Miles Davis. John Coltrane.'

'Oscar Peterson, Joe Pass?'

Cathy's eyes lit up. 'You like him? I heard him at Ronnie Scott's last year. He's great! Generally I like classical guitar though.'

'Hey, hear that, Dev? We've got us a little intellectual lady.'

Dev got up swiftly and threw the remains of his vodka into the collection of house plants decorating the fireplace.

'*Folk!* You heard her!' He was disgusted. 'What's wrong with rock? What's wrong with electric guitar?'

She was uneasy. 'Nothing. It just doesn't do as much. You know – not so many chord variations. But you're a musician, you know all about it. I don't know anything about rock, I told you. And folk's okay. It's simple and true. Why are you sneering?'

'It's crap.'

'A friend of mine says it's the music of the ordinary people.' Cathy said, stiffly.

'Don't say you're into politics too!'

'Why not? I'm alive, aren't I?' She was hostile.

Dev said, 'How can you have simple, true music, when the world is upside down and everything complicated? It's not true at all, it's a lie! We've got to find a new kind of music, not look back. You know Miles used electronic instruments, effects?'

'Yes,' said Cathy. 'I didn't say . . .'

'At the moment we don't know what to do with our electronics, but we're learning. You know that an electric guitar really switched over can blow your mind, baby? You know the effects you can get by playing into the amplifiers? You know the same phrase played over and over, a certain vibration, can act like a mantra? There's a different kind of music coming now. With electronics we might even go beyond it one day . . .'

Cathy stared at him. His face looked quite different now. Alive, younger. He was talking enthusiastically, his highly creative intelligence making her see, briefly, the vision *he* saw.

19

He was so beautiful.

The thought must have been mirrored in her eyes, because suddenly, he stopped talking, and it was as though a curtain had risen. He was looking at her quite differently now.

She realized, fully, for the first time, how devastatingly sexy and attractive he was. Not just coldly beautiful. Her breath seemed to go away, and the colour flooded up and burned deeper in her pale skin. She was too young to be able to stand that kind of looking. She turned away, swallowing.

His experience of girls was wide. He read her clearly, seeing the bewildered flare of desire. He smiled mockingly, disappointed. So he hadn't been mistaken. A nice little actress, pretty as a peach, with a maggot in the centre, like the other one.

Cathy was shaken and confused. She could not understand the lightning changes of mood, and she could not understand the emotional tension between them. With Chris too. Why had Dev looked at her like *that*? A perfectly ordinary afternoon had turned into something like an eerie surrealist film.

'Dev,' said Chris, coolly. 'The law's here.'

Cathy relaxed as the panda car stopped on the gravel outside the open door.

A moment later, James Harlow, the village bobby, came into the hall, hesitant, taking off his cap, so that the sun caught his fair hair.

'You took your time!' Dev spun round and walked over to him.

Jim's colour rose. 'I'm sorry, sir. I got here as quickly as possible. There was an urgent call, just as I was setting off. What seems to be the trouble?'

'Nothing *seems* to be the trouble. There *is* trouble. I spent god knows how much making this place secure and private. We got back from our U.S. tour today, *today*, you understand, and what do I find? A bloody girl has got in already! She couldn't just have wandered on to the property. I want her arrested for breaking and entering!'

That very morning Jim had had a telephone call from his Chief, who had told him who the new tenant of Cox's Farm was, and given strict orders that Jim must keep an eye open for fan trouble, *and* keep Devlin sweet. 'I don't want any trouble, d'you hear me, Harlow?' he went on. 'Especially I don't want any trouble with the Press.

Anything of that nature and we'll have a small riot on our hands. Once they know he's here the fans will start arriving. I don't want it. I can't spare the men to help you. His manager says he wants absolute privacy. *Understand?*'

Jim understood very well indeed. Blow this, and he might never get promotion again, anywhere. The telephone call had realized his worst fears.

'Where ...?'

'Over there.'

He looked round. There was a girl with a wild mane of tangled gold hair, long arms and legs. Brief, too brief, clothes, clinging wetly to her. She smiled ruefully.

'Hello, Jim.'

He went white. 'Good grief, Cathy! What are you doing *here*? Mary was wondering where you were.'

'I was painting in the water-meadow by the stream, and he came along and made me come back here. He thinks I'm after him, a groupie, or something. They're pop stars, I think.'

Chris, glancing from one to the other, started to laugh helplessly. But Dev hardly moved.

'You know her?'

'She's my sister, sir. Down here from London. Staying at the Police House with us for a couple of weeks' holiday.'

'She broke in.'

'Cathy, how did you get in? I told you Cox's Farm is sealed off and private now.'

'There's a gap in the Police House hedge. I just walked through it.'

Chris gave another yelp of laughter. The Police House was actually built in one corner of the Farm property. It was one of the reasons Dev had bought the place. It was the only section they hadn't bothered to electrify.

'I wanted to paint by the edge of the stream. There's that old tree, you remember. And you said that nobody was here, only the couple who look after the place.'

'But what happened? You're wet, and you look ...'

She flushed. 'I fell in the stream. There were cows – no, bullocks ...' Her eyes slid to Chris, and she bit her lip, trying not to laugh.

'It isn't funny, Cathy!' Jim was annoyed. He turned to Dev. 'Look,

I'm very sorry, sir. I think there's been a real misunderstanding. You can see for yourself what happened. My sister is very wrong to be here, but she's only just come down, and it used to be all open land. If you wish to press charges of course, I'll have to ...'

There was silence. Dev looked at her, his eyes glittering. How could he take it any further? It would never stand up in court. He thought of the publicity the media would stir up. He felt he could kill her.

She realized that he thought he had been made a fool of, deliberately. 'I'm sorry,' she said, hopelessly. 'You just wouldn't give me time to explain. You were so angry, I thought it would be better to just come along. If you let me go now, I promise I won't ever come back.'

He stared at her, dangerous.

'Dev!' said Chris, slowly and clearly. '*Dev!*'

'What is it?' He did not look away from her.

'Dev, it seems to me we may have been a little hasty ...'

Dev spun round, outraged, but whatever he read in Chris's eyes, stopped him dead. Cathy could see nothing.

'You don't want any local publicity, Dev. You'll have the fans down on you again. You'll have to sell the farm, and it took long enough to find it. You don't want to upset the local law –' he smiled at Jim – 'or the media boys. After all, Cathy has apologized. It seems to me we've been a little tough on her. You've been rude to her and frightened her. Wouldn't it be kind of friendly if you invited her to stay over and eat a meal with us this evening? To show there's no hard feelings on either side.' His voice was silky smooth.

Once again, Cathy was sure that some message passed between them, too subtle for an outsider to pick up. Suddenly, she was unreasonably panic-stricken. She could hardly wait to get away from them. They were *dangerous*.

Then Dev was laughing, recklessly, almost wildly.

'All right, Chris. It's your choice. You win.' He turned. 'What do you say, Cathy. You'll stay? We'll drop the charge if you stay and keep us company. We're lonely with no one around!'

Cathy gaped at him, her mind a blank.

'B-but you wanted to get rid of me just now! And I'm wet through, not dressed for ...'

'We can lend you something dry.'

Cathy saw that Jim was frowning at her. She tried to signal to him that she did not want to stay, but he only looked angrier.

'And my sister-in-law will have cooked a meal for me . . .'

'We'd appreciate your company. We like to relax with friends after a tour.' Dev's voice was steely.

Jim made up his mind. *Keep Devlin sweet!* 'I'll tell Mary you'll be late, Cathy. Mr Devlin's been very kind to overlook the matter, and even to invite you for a meal. I'm sure you're grateful. It's a big treat, you know!' He went over to Dev, and held out his hand. 'Thank you very much, sir, I appreciate your co-operation. I hope you'll enjoy a long and untroubled stay in this house. Cathy, give me a ring if you want a lift home.'

'Don't worry. I'll bring her back. My car's outside,' said Chris.

Dev went to the door with Jim and shook his hand again. A few seconds later the little car drove off with a spurt of gravel.

# Two

Cathy stood feeling stranded, her heart beating unpleasantly, and a stupid cold feeling like a foreboding rising in her spine. It was ridiculous to feel so deserted. It was only a meal. In an hour or so she would be home, and wild horses wouldn't drag her back to this place!

She felt Chris's gaze on her again. If only they wouldn't keep *looking*, she thought. If only she could stop the silent tension building up again. Perhaps, if she kept talking ... but she was too frightened of Dev – not only Dev. Why did they want her here? They already had at least one guest – the girl on the sofa, who had not moved or spoken since Jim came in.

Dev said to the girl, 'Go tell Mrs Kaye she can put the food in the garden room. We'll help ourselves.' The girl drifted out, making no comment, her eyes totally blank.

Cathy, looking at her, shivered, then sneezed and sneezed again. 'Look,' she said, 'I can't possibly stay. I haven't even got a tissue!'

Chris laughed.

'Baby's catching a cold,' said Dev, gently. He seemed to have got over his ill-temper.

'I'll take her up and give her a bath,' said Chris, getting up, grinning.

'Oh no, you don't. You'll catch her cold and we start the new album Monday. It'll be great having you croaking around ... She can come into my bath.'

Cathy swallowed. 'Look, I don't think ...' and she knew she had fallen into a trap when they both laughed.

They all three went upstairs. There was thick scarlet carpet everywhere, original paintings on palest green walls above mahogany panelling. She wanted to stop and look at the paintings but Chris put his arm round her shoulders and propelled her past.

24

'You can look at them tomorrow morning.'

She stopped dead. 'Tomorrow *morning?*'

'After breakfast.'

She blushed scarlet. 'Now look . . .'

'You know this little baby's getting on our wavelength pretty quickly, Dev.'

'Yeah,' he smiled sardonically. 'I guess so!'

She was trying not to show her panic. Although there was the appearance of joking, below there were strange undercurrents.

They stopped at a panelled door. 'The Guest Room,' said Dev, bowing mockingly. 'Invited or uninvited. Being a pop star, I have all my bathrooms en suite.'

She flushed. She said, 'Have you got something I could borrow? A sweater and jeans or something? Maybe that girl . . .'

'Charis didn't bring any luggage.' They looked at each other and laughed. 'A sweater and jeans? What do you think, Chris?'

'Certainly not. Being pop stars, Cathy –' (why did they find this so funny?) 'we prefer our women a little more decorative.'

'I noticed,' said Cathy, dryly. 'But I'm not one of your women, am I?'

'Aren't you?' Dev looked at Chris.

'No, I'm not!' Cathy was losing her temper. 'Just because you found me in the meadow like that, doesn't mean I'm a . . .'

'Groupie,' supplied Chris, grinning.

'Hooker,' countered Dev.

'A slag,' said Cathy, definitely. 'And you can stop patting me about like a mouse between two cats, or I'll walk straight out now and you can swear a complaint tomorrow.' She sneezed again. 'Are you going to give me something to wear, and let me wash, or am I going to get pneumonia?'

'You can have one of my shirts,' said Dev. 'They're big enough to cover you up. Come and choose one.'

Chris disappeared down the corridor, still laughing and they went across the corridor to Dev's room opposite. It was huge, with an enormous bed and thick carpets. It had a separate dressing room and bathroom, but Cathy was suddenly too tired and exhausted to take it all in. She sneezed again and stood shivering while he sorted through the dressing room cupboard, looking for something. She had never seen so many clothes together.

'This is the one.' Dev picked out a beautiful jade silk shirt. It was embroidered with purple and gold dragons. It had full sleeves and it wrapped around with a tie belt.

'It's beautiful,' said Cathy, holding it up to herself to test the length, and stroking the fabric.

Dev was staring at the shirt.

'I wore that at Madison Square Garden our first time in the States.' He laughed, slamming the door. 'Twenty thousand people going crazy. I don't think I've ever been so frightened in my life. It's never seemed as bad since.'

Cathy looked at him with respect. 'It must take a lot of nerve. It's a strange kind of life.'

'Yeah, just you and forty thousand people who want to see your pants split.'

'Some of them must be there for the music,' said Cathy unsympathetically, going to the door. 'You're lucky you can do what you want to do. Imagine the jobs some people have. Are you sure you want me to wear this special shirt? Anything would do, you know.'

His eyes gleamed. 'I knew it would suit you, and this is a special occasion, isn't it?'

She opened the door, not bothering to reply.

'Oh, Cathy?'

She turned, reluctantly. 'Don't drown yourself in the bath. Being pop stars, all our baths are sunken!'


He wasn't joking. A few minutes later, Cathy was in the most magnificent bath she had ever used – or was ever likely to use, she thought. It was circular, six feet across, made in white marble, and sunken into a deep pile carpet of rose pink. It had gold taps and the water came out rose-scented.

She scrubbed off the mud with creamy soap made in the shape of a rose and, the fragrant steam around her, tried to relax, allowing the tiredness to drain away. The shivering went too, and she began to feel that she might be able to cope with the strain of the evening. She was not quite sure what she should be prepared for, but all her instincts warned her that something was *wrong*. She was almost too tensed up to enjoy all this fantastic luxury.

The towels were twice as thick as the towels at home, and she covered herself with the delicious after-bath lotion and talc, rubbing the talc into her cut feet to take away the stinging. She must remember to go back for her sandals and the painting on the way home.

There were brushes and combs and tissues on the mirrored dressing bench, and she sat down, with a sigh of relief, to brush her hair free of its tangles, into its usual satin-gold. Then she slipped on the shirt. It had a spicy, exciting smell. Its smooth silk was warm against her skin, and she felt strange, as though she was being touched. It was too big across the shoulders, but, well, she wouldn't be appearing at Madison Square Garden. She giggled. It was reasonably long – longer than her shorts had been. It seemed to plunge rather more than she liked. She looked for a safety pin in the glass bowl, but found only hair pins.

Looking at the shirt in the mirror, with its oriental pattern, she had a new idea. She combed out her hair again and began pinning it up securely into a neat pleat at the back of her head, as she often did when she was working.

Before she was finished, there was a knock on the door, and Dev's voice told her he was going down, and she was to come down when she was ready.

She drew a deeper breath, and pressed another pin into place with fingers that trembled ever so slightly. Why did he have this effect on her? Why was she so frightened of him? After all, he had only shouted at her a little, and pushed her around a bit. Perhaps it was the way his moods and temper seemed so out of control. There seemed to be a wild desperation beneath the surface. She did not know what he would do next. It was a good thing Chris was around. He seemed to be able to handle him. But how reliable was Chris? She remembered he had stopped her walking out when Dev was away.

She looked in the mirror and had to smile. The effect was just what she wanted! Goodbye, nature girl, with disturbing suggestions of availability. The smooth, pinned-up hair gave an air of coolness and remoteness. Her skin, flushed from the bath, looked delicate and fragile, like a very breakable porcelain figure. Well, they liked their women decorative, not functional. She laughed aloud. She stuffed tissues into her belt and went resolutely down the stairs to the room where she could hear music and voices. No good putting it off any longer.

She drew a deep breath and walked in.

From the noise she had expected other people in the room, but there was only Dev, Chris and the girl, Charis, lying on her back on a sofa reading another magazine. Cathy wondered briefly if she ever did anything else.

There was an odd silence, quickly covered by Dev, telling her to help herself to food on the side table. She turned away, feeling shy of their intense gaze on her, and concentrated on getting the food. She found fresh salmon, salad, several kinds of cooked meats, butter and crusty home-made bread. Suddenly she felt very hungry. With her neat, deft movements, she quickly collected a plate of food, and a fork, and went across the room to join them.

It was another beautiful room, pale green and soft gold. There were deep sofas by the long windows open to a paved terrace and the new, softly lit swimming pool, with the warm twilight garden beyond. In front of the sofas were strangely shaped glass tables, glowing softly and changing colour every few minutes. Light sculptures. There were large, low lamps, too, and in one corner, a fantastically complicated piece of equipment, which she supposed must be some sort of sound and video system. On the adjoining wall was the largest collection of records and cassettes she had ever seen, like a library, from floor to ceiling.

She sat down and began to eat ravenously, watching the light sculptures. She had counted up to eight separate colour combinations, when she became aware of the quality of the silence.

'Ninety-six,' said Chris, gently. 'I made them.'

She glanced sideways and found they were watching her, very serious, *predatory*. Her heart bumped unpleasantly.

Dev had changed into a pair of scarlet velvet trousers and a narrow black silk shirt, which hung negligently open, revealing his tanned, muscular chest, and the strange stone pendant on a thin cord, which she had noticed before.

'What's the matter? Why are you watching me?' She was surprised to hear her voice, more tense and defiant than she had intended.

28

'We like watching you.'

'Don't you like watching *us*?'

Cathy went red and looked away.

'Where's our little baby gone, though?' Chris sounded plaintive. He was crunching his way through a loaf.

'Baby's grown up and turned into Madame Butterfly.' Dev's eyes moved over her, slowly, caressingly, as though he was touching her, and Cathy's mouth went dry. He was looking at her as he had looked just before Jim had arrived. She found she could not breathe properly.

She stood up and said, breathlessly, 'Do you mind if I get a second helping?'

'Help yourself.' He sounded cool.

Cathy said, trying to be friendly and casual, 'Do you want anything?'

There was silence, and she was forced to look at him again. He smiled slowly. Their eyes locked, and suddenly, helplessly, the colour was flooding up her neck, burning deeply and vividly under her skin. She closed her eyes in anguish.

'Dev isn't eating *food*, tonight!' Chris said, dryly, and Cathy was able to smile shakily. Thank heavens for Chris.

Dev stretched tautly, and got up. He laughed. 'That's right. I'm drinking though. Do *you* want anything?'

But she refused to look at him, and said, over her shoulder, 'I don't drink much, thanks.'

'There's some Coke here.'

'All right.'

'You're destroying the image,' said Chris. 'Coke is Suzie Wong, not Madame Butterfly. Give her some saké.'

Dev laughed. 'That's a good idea. Have we got any?'

'We've got everything.'

Cathy turned. 'Thanks, but I don't ...' and found Dev right behind her. He gave her a full glass, making her fingers touch his. Her hand and arm tingled and her heart was hammering against her ribs.

'Coke, with a little something else.'

She kept her head bent so that he should not see how much she was disturbed by his closeness and touch. He laughed, very softly,

29

knowing exactly the effect he was having on her, and then, very slowly, he put his fingers on the nape of her neck and stroked it gently. She felt unable to move, drowned in sensations she had never experienced before.

'You're beautiful, little baby. Beautiful.'

Chris said, loudly, 'It's time Baby was converted to rock. Dev, put on a record – one of ours.'

At the sound of his voice she was able to move away quickly, to sit by him, her face burning.

There was a dangerous silence. Suddenly Dev was shockingly, furiously angry. 'You bastard!' he said, softly. 'You bloody bastard! Put it on yourself!' He hurled the full glass he was holding, across the room and through the open french windows, to smash in fragments out on the terrace. Then he stalked out after it. There was a dark stain on the pale carpet. Cathy found her hands were shaking.

A security guard in a grey uniform came in quickly from the house, someone she had not seen before.

'It's all right. Leave it. Tell Gus. Dev just blew his top!' Chris was laughing. The man grinned, shrugged his shoulders and went out.

Cathy pushed her plate away. 'W-what's the matter with him? And you too. Why are you all wound-up like this?'

He got up, poured two drinks, put one down in front of her, and sat next to her. 'We got back today. We haven't slept for forty-eight hours. I don't think Dev's slept or eaten since the last concert in Los Angeles. He never does. It takes him weeks to get over one of these trips. Sixteen weeks we've been in the States. Twenty-seven major concerts, audiences forty thousand – sixty thousand. Travelling all day between times. We're stretched out like skinned pigs.'

Appalled, she stared at him. 'B-but how do you manage to keep going?'

'There are traditional comforts.'

'Comforts?'

'Booze, women, dope. What's the matter?'

'Drugs.'

'It's all right. Don't get worried. We're mostly straight now. We came off the stuff two years ago when Keith Hurst, our drummer, got a heroin habit. The band nearly fell to pieces. We kept getting usted. Copenhagen, Rio, Hong Kong, even when we hadn't got any!' He laughed bitterly. 'It got expensive buying our way out. We decided the game wasn't worth it. It took Keith a year to shake it. He's all right now. Married. Lives in Edgware.'

He poured more drinks. 'People don't understand about the sheer boredom and loneliness. You travel all day. You get to the venue. You play. Your energy level is sky high. Then it's over. There's nothing to do but go back to the hotel. And the next day it's the same again. Car, plane, car, concert, hotel room, over and over again. Sometimes there's a break of a day or so, and then you sleep, or try to. After a while you can't sleep because you're too screwed up. And you're bored, *bored*.'

She stared at him.

'Then there's the loneliness. No one ever believes that. But it's true.'

She looked at him doubtfully. 'But what about all those girls . . .'

'Oh sure! There are plenty of girls if you want them for the night. Or others, like lil' ol' Charis, there. Rich ladies wanting kicks.' They looked at her. She seemed completely lost. Her head lolled sideways on the arm.

'But you know, Cathy, when you get older you want something different. Something genuine, permanent. But it's difficult. Our bass player, Leo Field, has been married since he was sixteen. He's got a real home and a couple of kids. We all envy him.'

He stared out into the dusk, his face suddenly sad.

'The trouble with Dev is that he can't relax at all. He never could. We went to school together. We've always been friends, closer than brothers. He can't sleep. He can't eat. He never liked drugs much. Says they stop creative ideas coming through, and he doesn't like the sort of girls who follow the bands. Two years ago, he had this really bad scene with . . . well . . . a rich bitch. Crazy about her. Even wanted to marry her, but she was playing. Only wanted him around as a status symbol. It took a lot to keep her quiet – all his creative energy. He never wrote anything for half a year. That's when the band nearly fell apart. He's lead guitar, you know. He writes the music. I do the vocals, and write the words, sometimes.'

'How long have you been . . . living, like this?'

'Seven, eight years. Since we hit the big time.'

31

'He'll have a breakdown,' said Cathy. 'Perhaps he's having now. I don't understand how he's still functioning.'

'You saw. He drinks vodka, lives off his nerves. Explodes int violence, mostly in his music.'

She shivered. 'He frightens me.'

Chris looked at her defensively. 'He isn't always like this. Yo should see him on stage. He's good. We all are.' He thought. 'Very very good.'

'But why do you do it? You must have enough money.'

He shrugged. 'It's a great life when you're nineteen, poor, and ma about music. You want girls, money, fame. It's only later that thing change. The legend begins to own *you*.' He looked at her seriously 'You know we're quite normal, Cathy. When we're home we're a right. Basically we are musicians who got caught up in the bally-hoo, the publicity the media dreams up. It turned us into a commercial product. You start to live up to the image the media invents for you. You become a mini-industry, instead of a band.'

'That's what I don't like about the pop scene,' said Cathy. 'It all seems like a put on. I keep asking myself: Do they really mean that, or is it just to sell the record. I need to know something is real and true.'

She looked at the girl Charis, stretched out now, eyes closed, but somehow not asleep. 'Nothing's real for her any more. She's a living dead person.'

He shrugged. 'Don't worry about her. She's having a nice little trip.' He grinned. 'But don't tell your brother. He wouldn't like it.'

She shivered. 'I've got to go.'

'Look, I'll play you our latest album. It's not released yet. See if you dig it. See if it's real and true enough for you. The music is what we are all about really. Everything else is hype.'

'All right.' She relaxed, and drank the third glass he had poured for her. She began to feel better, reckless, light-headed.

The music, rude, loud, aggressive, totally alive, split the quiet air. The bass and drum, heavy, pounding, then a guitar, weaving and writhing, played very fast by a virtuoso, then a voice, in the tradi-tion of the blues, shouting out, destroying comfortable hypocrisies.

'That's you!' she said, delightedly. 'You sound like Robert Johnson.'

He laughed. 'I wondered if you'd get it. I was a blues shouter with one of the old R and B groups when I was at school. I was into jazz in a big way before I joined up with Dev again. Never thought rock would get me ...'

'This isn't just rock,' she said, puzzled. 'It's like well, it's everything: rhythm and blues, a bit of jazz, bit of reggae, soul. And you've got electronics in there too, somehow. It's all blended together into a new music. Yes, okay, it's real.'

He was looking at her, smiling, so that a comfortable warmth filled her. She was listening carefully. 'Muddy Waters, too ... No. That other man, Elmore James. And B. B. King I think. I'm not too hot on blues.'

He took her hand and held it. 'B. B. King. Cathy, I've fallen in love with you! Will you marry me?'

She laughed. 'How many other wives have you got?'

'None that can tell me about B. B. King!'

'That's a useful qualification for a wife?'

'I guess you've got others.' For a moment, his eyes went to her mouth, and when they reached her eyes again, they were serious and tense.

'I'm not joking, you know.'

She looked at him, stunned.

'You going to tell me about *my* influences, Cathy?'

Dev was leaning against the glass doors, looking at them both. She wondered, panicking, how long he had been there and what he had heard. Blushing furiously she pulled her hand away from Chris, and went over to the hi-fi, pretending to look at the album sleeve. As she reached for it, the music changed and she laughed.

'Oh I know that! We were all mad about it when I was thirteen. It's *Big Hopper* by the Connection.'

She picked up the album sleeve to look at the first record.

*Head Start, Easy Connection.*

Disbelieving, she gripped the sleeve cover and felt the blood draining away from her heart. She felt dizzy. It just couldn't be. Even *she* knew Easy Connection. *Everybody* knew Easy Connection, even if they had never heard a pop song in their lives.

They were, perhaps, the wildest of all the groups. They were younger than the great superstar rock bands, but counted as one

of them. As famous as the Stones, crazier than the Who, they ha
sold more records than the Beatles. They were more mysteriou
than Led Zeppelin had ever been. They never gave interviews, neve
appeared on television. Their fantastic concerts were sold out week
in advance. They were the centre of a huge cult following at th
universities and art schools, as well as appealing, no one quit
knew why, to the average pop fan. They were disapproved of by
politicians, parents and teachers. Questions had been asked abou
them in Parliament. They were reputed to be millionaires many
times over, and like Led Zeppelin, spent most of their time in th
United States. They had their own aeroplane and a police escor
everywhere they went.

And their scandals rocked the popular press – hotel scandals
fighting scandals, girl scandals, police raids, drugs . . .

It could not be true! Surely she would have known their *names*
*Recognized them.* And yet she could not remember seeing a close-up
picture of them. They never appeared on the covers of their albums
Her mind racing, she realized that she did not know the individual
names of Motorhead, Police, Genesis, or . . . well, dozens of other
bands. But it was all so incredible! Why should they be *here*, in a
tucked away bit of countryside? Surely there would be guards,
managers . . . but there *had* been a guard. Maybe more than one
even.

She drew a deep breath and turned and looked at them.

Dev had sat down next to Chris and they were both half-sitting,
half-lying, as they had earlier, resting their heads against the sofa
back, looking at her from weary, half-closed eyes.

She could not relate the roaring legend to these quiet, exhausted
young men, with their strange austere beauty, and yet she had felt
all along that they were dangerous.

'Y-you're the Connection? Easy Connection?' She still could not
believe it.

Dev said, 'As if you didn't know.'

Chris ignored him and said, slowly, 'It worries you?'

She nodded, looking young, sick, shaken. 'Yes, it worries me.'

'You remember what I said?'

'Yes, but . . .'

Their eyes met. *But.* He knew what that meant, and he read in er eyes a kind of wariness, almost fear, which had not been there earlier. If she had begun to feel anything for him, it had withered away, too new and fragile to withstand the scorching public image of the Connection. She was too young to understand the distortions of the media. In any case she didn't want to know. She just wanted to keep clear of trouble and not get herself dirtied up.

In which case she ought to be running like hell for the Police House, if she was reading Dev's intentions right.

'We're the good ones!' he protested, trying to joke.

He had said he wanted something different, thought Cathy. No wonder it was difficult. She understood now. Who would want to get involved with Easy Connection, even if they weren't as bad as they were painted? Their bad reputation brushed off on to everybody.

'I think I ought to go.'

Chris said, bleakly, 'You're judging us from newspaper reports.'

'I'm not judging you. I don't know anything about you. If I'd known you were so famous I'd never have stayed. This isn't my kind of scene at all. Your world is so strange and unreal.'

'That's another judgement. How do you know it's unreal?' His disappointment had turned to a slow anger. 'It's maybe more real and alive than yours.'

'I mean, it's unreal to *me*. I can't imagine what it would be like to have unlimited freedom, unlimited money. You can do pretty well whatever you want, can't you?'

'Are you saying we have no morals?'

'I don't know. Have you?'

Dev smiled, slowly, devastatingly. 'They're on flexitime.'

There was a long silence. They continued to watch her, through half-closed eyes, not moving, and that terrible, speaking tension was back, building between the three of them.

Then Dev began to laugh. He looked sideways. 'Chris . . . ?'

'No.'

'Ol' buddy . . .'

'Still no. *I* found her.'

'I spoke to her first.'

'She smiled at me.'

'I touched her first.'

35

'I kept her here.'

'Droit de Seigneur!'

'Finders Keepers!'

They burst out laughing. It was a ritual, a game they had played many times before.

There was a brief silence, and then Dev said slowly, in quite a different tone of voice. 'It's a power play, Chris.'

Chris shrugged and grinned, stretching his legs out. 'It's been a long time. She's too young.'

'Share?'

Chris shook his head regretfully. They stared at her. Dev said slowly, not taking his eyes away from her. 'All right. I'll trade.'

There was such a long silence, that Cathy looked up and saw Chris staring at Dev, his face absolutely blank.

'You're kidding.'

'No.'

*'Trade?'* He sounded shaken.

'Right.'

At last Chris said, almost casually, 'Okay, if you're sure. I'm willing.'

There was a powerful surge of exhilaration from Dev. He bounced up from the sofa, put on more music, poured more drinks.

Cathy looked from one to the other, not understanding. She was very frightened. She should have made a fuss and gone home with Jim. Her instinct had been right. Here were these two at the end of their rope, reckless. Dev at least had been drinking vodka all day, although he gave no sign of being drunk. They were used to taking chances, making all kinds of mischief. *What kind of deal had they made?*

She heard her voice, breathless. 'I want to go home.'

'Chris, she wants to go home!'

'She's heard about our bad reputation, Dev!'

They laughed, almost hysterically.

'Come and dance, Cathy, and I'll take you home.' Dev held his arms out.

She backed away. 'No, please, I'd rather go now.'

'A drink for the road then.'

She took the full glass, and drank the pale liquid down quickly, feeling it burn like fire.

'Have another.' She drank that too, feeling desperate. Anything to get away. She was aware of a strange floating sensation. Her knees felt weak. She thought, dazed, 'I'm getting drunk.'

Dev was looking at her in that dark, intense way, and she felt dizzy. Her heart began to race in her throat. He put his arms around her and drew her close.

There was the same electrifying explosion of sensation that she had felt before. Suddenly, uncontrollably, she was trembling all over. She put her hands to his shoulders trying to push him away. She had never felt like this with anybody before.

'You don't want to go. Stay with me, little baby,' he said softly. She tried to pull away, looking at Chris, but he stared back, grave, neutral, and she realized she could expect no help from him now. They had made some kind of deal and *he had handed her over to Dev.*

The panic rose again. 'Let me go. Please, I'm not like that ...'

'Like what?' He held her closer, hard against his body. There was a strange unreality now, like a dream, or a nightmare. If only she hadn't drunk so much. She tried to focus on something to stop the trembling, and saw the finely carved stone, hanging from a thin cord against his skin. It was a convex oval, with strange creatures, flowers and symbols, climbing up round it in a spiral.

'That's beautiful.'

'You like my stone? It's a wishing stone. I brought it from Mexico. An old man gave it me. He says it came from Atlantis, the lost continent. You have to rub it three times against your heart, and three times against the place of your mystic third eye in the middle of your forehead. Like this. Then you kiss the stone and wish.' He demonstrated, and closed his eyes. She wondered what he had wished. He surely had everything anyone could want.

He drew her silk shirt aside a little and rubbed the stone three times against her heart, and then, three times against her forehead. Then he pressed the stone against her lips.

'Wish, Cathy, wish!' He was laughing recklessly.

Her thoughts whirled chaotically. Dev ... To paint well, she thought, suddenly clear. To paint really well and be a famous artist.

The whirling stopped. She put up her hand to push the stone away from her mouth, and the thin cord, entangled in their fingers, parted.

37

'Oh, I'm sorry. That's my fault.' She looked at him.

Dev was staring transfixed, at the stone loose in his hand. He looked at her blankly.

'Oh dear,' Chris's mocking voice. 'What *have* you done? Our Dev is very superstitious. It's his Celtic ancestors.'

'W-what's the matter? What have I done?'

'Broken the cord that binds. Go on, Dev, tell her the legend!'

But Dev continued to stare blindly at the stone.

Chris said, laughing. 'A baby for a bride wishing on the stone on her wedding night. A son if the cord that binds is broken.'

There was a strange silence. Cathy's mouth was dry with fear, and this other terrible emotion, which she could not identify. She tried to laugh, hearing the nervous shaking of her voice.

'It's a good thing it's not my wedding night!'

Dev's eyes looked down into hers. Strange, glittering. His voice was soft, stranger still. 'Perhaps it is.' Very slowly he began to remove the pins in her hair, one by one, dropping them on to the carpet, until her hair was floating free.

She stood under his hands, frozen, unable to move. He drew her close again, lifted her chin, and began kissing her lips, softly, lightly.

She pulled her mouth away, but her legs were so weak she needed his support. She could not meet his eyes, and she had forgotten Chris.

'Please, I've got to go. Please take me home. I think I've drunk too much.'

He looked at her, his eyes veiled, enigmatic.

'All right. It's time. We'll go this way, through the garden.'

She stopped at the garden doors, seeing the shattered fragments of glass on the terrace. 'I can't, I've no shoes.'

He picked her up as he had done earlier and carried her over the glass, along the terrace, and down the steps into the garden. She saw that they were at the side of the house, in the old apple orchard, instead of the side leading to the gateway.

'Why have we come this way?'

She heard him laugh recklessly. The cool, rose-scented air made her feel giddy. She *had* drunk too much. The apple tree branches swung crazily above her as he put her down in the shadows. He was kissing her again, heavy, deep kisses now, and she was gasping, quivering, her body awakened and aflame, but when she felt his hands on her she understood at last.

'No!'

He laughed breathlessly, pulled away her shirt, and pressed her hard against the tree trunk with his body. She began to struggle. She tore at his arms and hands, tried to move her knee to kick him, but he was too close. The muscles in his arms and shoulders were like iron and she could not stop him. She tried to cry out – surely the security guard would come. The breath tore soundlessly in her throat.

He was angry now. 'Stop it! Stop it, do you hear? It's what you came for, isn't it?'

She bit his lip hard, feeling his warm blood spurt in her mouth. She slashed at the skin of his back and shoulders with her nails. But it was too late, and he was too strong, too obsessed. 'Don't play that game! Stop it!'

His hands were greedy and bruising. His face above her in a shaft of moonlight was a silver demon mask, with black, hollow mouth and glittering eyes. She struggled, terrified, and cried out at the sharp pain as he forced roughly into her.

Later the pain and the demon mask were gone. She was lying in the long grass and he was kissing her. His body and hands were caressing, sensual, infinitely gentle now, and her traitor body was beyond her control. It was moving, dissolving into waves of ecstasy. Shameful, hateful, ecstasy.

Afterwards she lay, clinging to him helplessly, shuddering and crying. Ashamed. Dirty and ashamed.

'Sweet little baby!' he was saying, incredulously, like an echo in her mind. 'Sweet little baby!' His mouth was soft, trembling against her. 'Sweet little baby.'

At last it was over. He lifted her to her feet, his arms around her, holding her close, protective.

She was hurting, dazed, unable to believe what had happened to her. The bitter taste of his blood burned sickeningly at the base of her tongue. When he said, 'Cathy, did I hurt you? I didn't know it was the first time . . .' she turned away and was violently sick into the grass, holding the tree, retching miserably. Even when her stomach was empty, retching to get rid of the feelings of shame and defilement. But the taste of blood would not go.

He held her, murmuring, but she did not hear. She was alone in a black, howling, wilderness.

At last she was able to move. With an immense effort, she stood away from him, pulled the shirt round her and without looking back, walked away from him.

'Cathy . . .'

*'Don't touch me.'*

'Cathy . . .'

'Leave me alone!'

She began to run then, blind and desperate.

# Three

At the Police House, Cathy limped round to the back door and went into the kitchen. Mary, her sister-in-law, was washing-up.

'I didn't hear a car. I thought Jim said they were going to drive you back. He's had to go over to Bilston.'

'I . . . walked.'

'Fancy having dinner with the Connection! It'll be a nuisance having them in the village though. A lot of extra work for Jim.' She wiped her hands and turned, smiling. 'Now, tell me all . . .' The smile disappeared. 'What on earth are you wearing?'

'I fell in the stream. They lent me a shirt.'

'But look at your feet! They're *bleeding*! Where are your sandals?'

For the first time Mary saw the look on Cathy's face and her strange, wild eyes. She came to her quickly.

'What happened? What did they do to you?'

'Don't, Mary. Don't touch me.'

Mary's face went white. 'Cathy! They didn't . . . Surely they didn't . . . ?'

'It was Dev. I drank too much. He made me do it.' Her voice sounded like winter.

Mary's hand went to her mouth. 'Oh my God!'

'I couldn't stop him.' She was trembling.

'I'll phone Jim. He's got to come back immediately.'

'*No!*' Her voice rose to a hoarse scream. '*No*. He mustn't know. No one must know. Nobody at all. I couldn't bear it.'

'Cathy! You've *got* to . . .'

'*No!* Please, Mary . . . can't you understand how I feel?' Suddenly, the icy blankness dissolved and she stretched out her hands to Mary, childlike, the tears running down her cheeks.

'Help me, Mary. Please help me. I feel so dirty.'

Mary's face twisted and she put her arms round Cathy quickly,

41

and held her tightly, comfortingly, allowing the tears to flow. Allowing the shock to ease. At last the storm of crying died down, and Mary took her upstairs, sat her on her bed and got a glass of brandy from the medicine cupboard.

Cathy drank it obediently, her teeth chattering on the glass. She could not stop shivering.

'I must wash.'

'Yes, yes, in a minute.'

'Oh, Mary, I can still feel him. I must get rid of this dirtiness. This filthy shirt!' She struggled out of the shirt and crumpling it up, hurled it away from her, burying her face in her hands. Mary got her dressing gown and put it around her. She was shocked at the livid bruises beginning to show on the delicate skin.

'We ought to get a doctor. Are you torn?'

'No. It wasn't like that. I'll be all right. I don't want a doctor.' The brandy was beginning to work. Her voice sounded more controlled.

'Tell me about it, Cathy.'

Drearily, Cathy told her everything, from the time her painting had fallen over. When she had finished there was a long silence.

Mary said, a cold anger in her voice. 'Cathy, you've got to tell Jim. That man has got to be prosecuted. He mustn't be allowed to get away with it. It's not right.'

Cathy shook her head. 'Mary, you're not thinking straight. Don't you see, we can't do anything?' She laughed bitterly. 'Oh, he knew what he was doing all right. He had it planned right from the start, when he asked me to stay to a meal. He knew we wouldn't be able to do anything. It was to pay me back for making him look such a fool.'

'We've got to do *something* . . .'

'How can people like us do anything? He's rich and *famous*. His money and lawyers would get him off. Can you imagine what they'll say about me? All the newspapers would report it. They'd say I was an easy girl, chasing after the famous star, probably after his money, a pay-off. Or that I was crazy and hysterical and nothing happened at all. Or, maybe they'd say I got drunk, which is true, and if I was a good girl, I'd have kept away from dangerous groups like Easy Connection.'

'There's the scandal,' said Mary. 'They wouldn't like that.'

Cathy laughed again. 'You think they'd worry about that? It all helps their image! *I'm* the one who would be branded. I'm the one people would whisper about behind their hands. I couldn't stand it. I wouldn't be able to go to College. Everybody would know!' Her voice rose again. 'I'd rather be dead!'

It was so unlike the normally practical Cathy that Mary was frightened.

'Cathy don't. You mustn't ever say that. Nobody knows about it except me.'

'Promise you won't tell anyone. *Promise*. On your sacred oath.'

Mary hesitated, but the look in Cathy's eyes decided her.

'I promise I won't tell anyone if you don't want me to. I can understand how you feel, but I can't think it's right he should get away scot free.'

'It's no good, honestly. We can't do a thing. What about you and Jim? You know the trouble it would cause. The police would be furious at the publicity. The public would say it was the police persecuting poor old Easy Connection again, and it might even affect Jim's chance of promotion. In any case, he couldn't go on working here, next to Cox's Farm. You know he couldn't. You'd be transferred. And it took you so long to get this place. You love it here. You've built up your life here.'

Mary said violently, knowing that Cathy was speaking the truth, 'Jim should have brought you back instead of trying to keep Paul Devlin quiet. They must have thought he'd handed you over on a plate!'

Cathy said wearily, 'I suppose he thought they were just normal people. He didn't realize the state they were in. How much they'd been drinking. Mary, I must have a shower.'

'Yes,' said Mary, mechanically. 'But what are you going to do?'

'Don't worry. I'm sorry I've been such a trouble to you. Everything will be all right. But I can't stay here. I couldn't bear to see him again. I'll pack and go on the early train tomorrow, if you'll drive me to the station. I think there's a workmen's train at six-thirty.'

Suddenly Mary was crying. 'Oh Cathy! I'm sorry about all this. Just when things were going so well for you. You're so terribly young, and we're all the folks you have. I can't seem to think. I don't know what to do for the best. Where can you go?'

43

Cathy considered. 'I think I'll go along to the lodgings the College have fixed up for me, and ask if they can take me now. We start in two weeks anyway. And if that's no good, I'll ask my friend Carole if she can put me up for a while.'

'Have you got enough money?'

'I've saved a bit from my holiday job, and my grant should be coming through soon. I can manage.'

'I'll come up to town with you. I don't like the idea of you wandering around London with nowhere to stay.'

'Oh Mary. You're lovely, but Jim would guess something was wrong. What are we going to tell him? Remember you *promised* . . .'

'He won't be back tonight. He's helping to drag the river for a suspected suicide . . .'

Suddenly she began to shake. 'Cathy, *promise* me you won't . . .'

'No. I'll be all right if I can start my course. You can tell Jim that Carole phoned and asked me to stay – which is nearly true. She did invite me. He'll probably assume I'm angry because he made me stay at the Farm. *Don't worry.* I'll be fine. I'm used to looking after myself since Mum died. Aunt Cass was kind, but she wasn't really interested.'

'Cathy,' Mary was looking worried still, 'you *will* see a doctor, won't you? Just in case. You know, disease, or . . .'

Cathy looked away, feeling sick, 'Maybe. When I get to London.'

She went to shower, remembered the marble bath at Cox's Farm, and found she was crying again. Later, Mary brought up comforting warm milk, but it was a long time before she slept. Her memory played the track of the scene again and again. She twisted and turned, but it would not stop. It was not the struggle and the pain, which caused the mental agony. They remained in her mind, cold, *clean*. It was afterwards, the way her body had surrendered and loved him, which left her feeling disgusted and guilty. She slept at last with the taste of blood in her mouth.

Dev slept for the first time in four days, and woke after ten hours feeling released and well. It was as though a great weight had gone from him, and he had come out from underneath alive and new. He put out a hand for Cathy, remembered, and got up quickly.

He showered, grinning and cursing at the lacerations on his back and shoulders. Perhaps it was the violence which had allowed him to break through the log-jam of his own accumulated tensions and neurosis, that had been building up for two years. Now it was over, he realized how sick he had been. To break through and to find such sweetness was more than he could ever have hoped for.

He pulled on an old shirt and a pair of jeans and went out of the house quickly, into the brilliant morning. He heard the church clock in the village chime eight across the fields, as he walked swiftly down to the stream. He was sure, somehow, that Cathy would be there, waiting for him. He remembered the ecstasy and her helpless clinging, and he wanted her very much. She would surely be waiting. But the water meadow was empty.

He sat down and waited for a while, then prowled restlessly along the edge of the stream, watching the water running over the stones. Once he had wanted to paint something like this. Maybe it wasn't too late. Maybe *now* ...

She had left her sandals somewhere here. He smiled, remembering her indignation when he had picked her up and carried her over the gravel into the house. A captive, he had thought then. A bride, he thought now. He felt the Atlantis stone, its cord knotted and hanging round his neck again, and his heart lurched with a wild excitement. *A son.*

He crossed the stream and found the sandals, kicked carelessly on the muddy bank. As he bent to pick them up, he saw something in the bushes, gleaming pale in the sun. He pushed aside the bush and saw the painting propped against a tree. For a moment he stared, the elation draining away, and his pulse began to beat painfully. He picked it up. The paint was nearly dry, tacky when he touched it. The smell of fresh paint and turps came to him like an echo of the past. He saw that the painting was nearly completed.

A picture of the water and vegetation along the edge of the stream. In close-up the plants and leaves swayed and grouped themselves round an odd, dreamlike tree. The drawing was brilliant, the paint put on freshly, joyously. It was beautiful. She had done it in an afternoon, and that was some degree of concentration.

He drew a deep breath. No lies. All she had said was true. She was not a fan or a groupie. She had not known anything about him. Had not come because she wanted him. Had not lost her courage

at the last minute and been coy. Had not set out to tease him. She
had fought to stop him. No wonder she wasn't there to meet him.

He drew another deep breath and, feeling suddenly cold, turned
and walked back to the side gate, taking the painting with him. He
let himself out and walked along the lane to the Police House.

Mary came to the door in her apron, an egg slice still in her hand.
'Paul Devlin. I want to speak to Cathy.'

Mary stared at him. She went red, and then very white.

'I'm sorry, *Mr* Devlin, that's not possible.'

He looked at her silently.

'How *could* you . . . ?' She stopped, her eyes hard. 'No, that's a silly
thing to say. Rich, famous people like you don't have to worry about
people like us. You just stretch out your hand and take what you
want, and there's nothing to stop you . . .' Her voice trailed away,
trembling. 'She's only seventeen, Mr Devlin. Just starting out. She's
very sensitive and they say she's brilliant. A brilliant painter. Her
body's all bruises. What have you done to her mentally?'

He leaned against the door frame and smiled at her insolently.

'You want to see my bruises too? Just fetch her.'

She went red. 'She's not here. She's gone.'

'Don't be silly. This is Sunday. There are no buses and no trains
until 11.30.'

'I said she's gone, Mr Devlin. I don't tell lies.'

His face changed and he looked at her dangerously.

'When?'

'Six o'clock this morning.'

'Where?'

'I don't know. That's the truth too, so it's no good you looking
like that. Even if I knew I wouldn't tell you. She caught the workmen's train to London, and she'll have to find somewhere to stay
until the art college opens. We're all the folks she has, and now she
won't be able to come and stay with us here in case she runs into
you.' She blinked tears away. 'You had something to say to her, Mr
Devlin?'

'I've got something to say to her.' He started to walk away, then
turned back. 'I've got the painting she did yesterday. I'm buying it.
I'll send a cheque. You can let me know when you get her address.'

46

'Please, Mr Devlin, you know she won't want to sell it to you. Please leave us alone. We haven't anything you can't get elsewhere.'

'You've got Cathy,' he said and walked away, leaving her staring after him.

At Cox's Farm Chris was alone, eating breakfast and reading the newspaper.

Dev propped the painting on a chair and looked at it while he drank tea and ate toast.

Chris put the paper down, glanced at the painting and studied Dev.

'You look like you crawled out from under at last.'

'I have.'

'But, oh boy! look at those scratches, look at that swollen lip. What you been *doing* man?' The mockery in his voice changed. 'You bastard. You were supposed to bring her back. You let her go.'

'I had to. She tried to stop me. I lost my temper.'

The silence lengthened, and at last Dev met his friend's cold eyes.

'Couldn't you make it any other way?'

Dev flushed darkly. 'She fought me.'

'She was ready enough when she went out of here.'

There was another silence. 'She was a virgin, Chris. I hurt her.'

A muscle moved in Chris's jaw, but he said nothing.

Dev said, 'Tell me about yesterday.'

'You know.'

'I didn't believe it. That story about the bullocks, it was true?'

'She was painting. Absolutely concentrated. Then the bullocks came up, all curious and stood round in a half-circle.' He smiled. 'She tried to shoo them off, but got to laughing too much. They panicked, knocked the painting into the stream. She went in to get it, slipped on the stones and fell into the water. I thought she would swear or cry, but she sat on one of the stepping stones and laughed her head off. After that she got the painting out and put it in the shade to dry. Took off her shirt, wrung it out, put it over the bush to dry. Packed her painting gear. She was drying herself off in the sun when you came by.'

'But why didn't she say how she'd got in? Who her brother was?'

47

'You didn't give her a chance!'

'Oh Christ!' Dev put his elbows on the table and his head in his hands. 'I need a shrink. I'm getting paranoid. I thought – no I was *sure* she was some kind of boiler who'd thought up a new way of getting to us. Even after her brother came. Even last night. I thought she'd lost her nerve at the last minute.'

'You wanted to believe that.' Their eyes met. 'You wouldn't have got her any other way, would you? Not when she knew we were Easy Connection. You wouldn't listen to me either.'

Dev's eyes gleamed. 'You wanted her too. You'd have gone after her if I'd let her go. We know each other too well, ol' buddy. When I got her back to the house I was certain she was a fan. Whenever I looked at her she just came alight.'

'I saw her,' said Chris, sourly. 'What do you expect, when you were broadcasting sex at her like a computerized sound system on twenty thousand watts?'

'I didn't know I was.'

Chris snorted disbelievingly. 'Listen, is there a rape charge against you?'

Dev froze, and stared at him. 'Rape!'

'That's what it's called, man. Taken by force. R.A.P.E.'

Dev, suddenly pale under his tan, looked away.

'Well, it's something new!' Chris began to laugh. 'We never had one of those before. Drugs, debt, indecency, paternity orders, that little heiress we couldn't shake in Alabama . . .'

'Kidnap,' said Dev.

Chris laughed again. 'Yeah, that's right! But we never had a rape rap before. A policeman's sister, too! Sixteen years old, never been kissed. Clever old Dev! The media will have a field day with this one. I reckon you'll go inside this time. They've still got you on the books. There's the suspended sentence for the assault on the policeman in Middlesbrough.'

'I'd forgotten that,' Dev shrugged. 'She's seventeen, anyway.'

'She won't be, when the story hits the papers. She'll be *fifteen*, and below the age of consent, and everybody'll believe we've started in on little girls.' He laughed again.

'Shut up!' said Dev. 'It's not funny! I don't think she's making a complaint. She's gone.'

'Gone?'

'Run away to London this morning. I went down to the Police House and got a tongue-lashing from her sister-in-law. The sister-in-law knows. She went on about bruising, and how poor people like them are at the mercy of rich wicked guys like me. She won't tell me where she's gone.'

'What are you going to do now?'

'Find Cathy, of course.' Dev looked surprised. 'It shouldn't be difficult. She's a painter. The sister-in-law said she's going to art college. There aren't that number in London. From the standard of that painting it'll be one of the big ones.'

'What about our old Col?'

'Could be. I'll ring them tomorrow. Somebody's bound to be in the office. Lulabelle, probably. She'll give me the address if Cathy's a new student.'

Chris got up and looked at him directly.

'Listen, Dev. There's no trading on this one now. If I can take Cathy off you, I will.'

'I knew you'd renege on our deal, ol' buddy. When you thought about it. But I haven't given up.'

'She ran, didn't she? Looks like she gave *you* up!'

# Four

'I always like art students.' The landlady's small, hard eyes moved curiously over Cathy. 'They're not fussy about things, if you know what I mean.' It was a warning. Cathy's heart sank lower.

'It's good of you to let me come earlier,' she said, trying not to think of the rent, almost double the normal, paid in advance, which had eaten into her small savings – because of the high season, according to the landlady, although Cathy couldn't imagine any tourists willing to stay in this small, dark room overlooking a noisy street, in an out-of-the-way area. There was a divan, a chair, a table and a dirty cupboard smelling of stale food, with a gas ring on top. Everywhere needed a good clean.

'Well, I'm glad I had the room all nice and ready.' The landlady patted her fashionably cut, auburn-tinted hair complacently, her hand glittering with a large diamond ring. 'You can call me Diana, dear. Anything you need ...'

After she had gone, Cathy sat on the divan, trying not to feel depressed. She was lucky to have her own room. There were so many students in London, lodgings were like gold dust.

When she had got to Victoria yesterday, she had phoned her school friend Carole Muir from the station and had stayed overnight. Carole lived in a large house in Streatham, with doting parents. She had tried her best to persuade Cathy to stay longer. She was horrified when she saw the room.

'It's miles away from the College! They must be crazy! Why don't you stay with me for a while and we'll try to find something nearer?'

'It's hopeless, Carole. You know what it's like in London trying to find somewhere to live. The College lodgings officer said they had over fifty students still waiting.'

'I bet I'd find somewhere!' said Carole, rebelliously. She was a year older than Cathy, studying to be a teacher. She probably would, too, thought Cathy, wishing she had the same kind of self-confidence. But since Saturday, everything had seemed too much for her, too difficult.

She began to unpack half-heartedly. She would have to go over to Carole's tomorrow to pick up the rest of her cases. She looked out of the window, feeling miserable and incredibly tired, wishing she could go to sleep. But the divan, with its grubby candlewick bed-spread, was uninviting, and she remembered suddenly that there was nothing to eat or drink. She would have to go out to buy food and milk. Perhaps the air would be good for her. Later on, maybe, she'd feel more like cleaning up the room.

She put on her jacket and went down into the dusty street.

She took her time shopping, reluctant to go back to the gloomy little room, but when she got there, it was worse than she could have imagined.

*Dev was there.*

He was lying, stretched out on the divan, his hands behind his head, utterly relaxed, looking extraordinarily exotic in the dull room.

She went paper white, shut the door and leaned weakly against it, her eyes closed. She felt she was going to faint. She had never thought she would have to see him again.

His eyes moved over her, and a wild excitement gripped him. She was everything he had thought. She wasn't a figment of an ex-hausted, drunken dream. Fair, delicate-looking, slender, gentle. Large violet eyes, pointed chin, full soft mouth. He fought his desire down, and said softly, 'Hello, Cathy.'

The colour came back into her skin, a vivid burning scarlet, which seemed to engulf her face and all her body.

She walked past him and sat down with her back to him at the small table in the window. She gripped her hands together tightly. 'How did you get in?'

'Diana . . . obliged.'

'Jim told you I was here.'

'No. Mary said you were going to art college. I phoned round. Chris and I were both art students at the London. I know the people in the office. They gave me your address when I said I was buying your painting. Very impressed they were.'

51

He laughed.

'Your paints are over there in your bag. And your sandals, and clothes.' She remembered him lifting and carrying her, and the colour burned again.

His voice was very soft. 'Cathy, I found your painting in the bushes. I'm keeping it. There's a cheque on your desk.'

She picked it up curiously. It was for three hundred pounds. Her eyes went blank. Then she laughed harshly and tore it into small pieces, dropping them, almost casually, into the tin basket.

'You can keep the painting. You don't think I ever want to see it again, do you? There's no need for hush money. I'm not making a charge. You don't have to buy me off. I just want to forget it ever happened.'

He went white with temper, and got up swiftly. 'I'm not buying you off. I wanted the painting, but I'll send it back if I can't pay for it.'

'I don't want it.' She stared out of the window, not moving.

'Cathy, can't we talk?'

'There's nothing to say.'

There was a long silence. She waited, willing him to go. They could have nothing to say to each other. But the silence deepened and they were talking anyway, just as at Cox's Farm. Desperately, she closed her mind to him.

'Why did you come? What do you want?' He could hear the undercurrent of fear.

'You.'

She drew in her breath raggedly. 'Please go. I don't want you here. We haven't anything to say to each other.'

'I wasn't thinking of talking.'

She turned then, and looked at him fully for the first time. Her eyes were like black ice. 'You were thinking of another nice quiet little rape?'

'No,' his voice was even, his eyes unflinching as they met hers. 'I want the loving.'

She looked as though he had struck her. Her control broke and she spun away and put her face in her hands.

'Listen, Cathy. At first I really thought you were one of the groupies that follow us around. Then, later, I thought you were a

52

fan who wanted to go to bed with me, and maybe lost her nerve at the last minute. It sometimes happens, you know. They think of all sorts of ways of getting to you. When I found your painting, I knew I'd been wrong.'

Her voice sounded almost hysterical. 'Don't tell me you're apologizing. You're not saying you're sorry!'

He leaned against the desk, next to her, and putting his long hands under her chin, he forced her to look at him. He looked younger. The exhaustion, the desperation, had gone. His dark gold beauty was glowing with excitement. He was vividly alive.

'No, I'm not sorry. I wouldn't change what happened.' His voice softened. 'I'm sorry I hurt you, though. I didn't know you were a virgin.' There was laughter in his voice. 'There aren't many around in my business.'

Her colour burned brilliantly under his fingers. She could not look at him.

'It's just a joke to you!' Her voice was choked. 'But I always wanted it to be for real, the first time. With my husband or my true love. Not ... like animals, under a tree ...'

'That's how it was for you? All of it?'

She jerked her head away, and stood with her back to him.

'You wanted me before we went into the garden, Cathy. You wanted me a lot. I don't understand why you fought me, when you wanted it so much.'

Her voice was so low he could hardly hear it. 'I never felt like that before. You and Chris kept looking at me ... I drank too much. I couldn't think properly and you touched me. I *tried* to make you stop ...'

He laughed suddenly. 'That's true! See what you did to me!'

He unbuttoned his shirt and pulled it off.

The livid weals down his back shook her. There were deep scratches on his arms and shoulders too. Had she scarred him for life?

'What's the matter, Cathy? You look worried.' His voice was gentle and he drew her towards him.

'Will there be scars?'

'They'll go. What about you?' Without hesitation he lifted off her teeshirt. She turned her head away and closed her eyes. She made no attempt to struggle. She knew how much stronger he was. There was no one to stop him.

Her arms and breasts were discoloured with bruises. Some were turning an unpleasant purple. On her hips the skin had been broken.

He drew in a deep breath and touched her gently. Then he put both arms round her and held her against him, his cheek against her hair.

'Poor little baby, I really hurt you. Poor little baby. I'll make it up to you. I swear I will.'

He bent and kissed her breasts and then her mouth. 'Sweet little baby.' His voice was soft and gentle, caressing, reminding her of the night. 'Sweet little baby . . .' he had said then. The scent of the roses. Her body moving.

Suddenly she could taste his blood in her mouth again, nauseating. Her skin was very pale and a faint perspiration had broken out across her forehead.

'Let me go,' she said. 'I'm going to be sick!' She turned swiftly to the door, stumbling into the arms of the landlady just coming in. She thrust her aside and ran down the passage.

'Well!' said Diana, looking at him speculatively. 'W-e-e-e-l-ll . . . You are a fast worker, I'm sure.' Her eyes flicked over his bare chest. 'This is a respectable house. I don't know what the College is going to say. In the middle of the day, too! You students are all the same.'

He laughed and put on his shirt. 'We weren't.'

'As good as.'

'All right. How much?'

She bridled. 'I don't know what you mean. The University wouldn't like it. She's only young too.'

'I'll give you fifty quid. Don't talk to her about it. Do you hear me? Fifty pounds and you'll let me in here when I want. Is it a deal?'

Her eyes gleamed. 'Well, I'm not one to spoil young love. I wouldn't like to get her in bad with the College.'

'No. They might come down and find out what kind of a place you're keeping here.'

'Don't you talk dirty to me, or fifty pounds won't be enough.'

He smiled grimly. 'If you look after the girl and see she's all right,

you might find Santa Claus comes to town more often than once
a year.'

She looked at him narrowly. 'You're no student.'

'Not now.'

Down the corridor a door banged.

'There's Cathy. Clear off now and remember, I don't want her
bothered.'

She went off down the passage, the money he had given her
folded into the palm of her hand.

'Hello, love, feeling better now? Must be something you ate.'
Cathy averted her eyes and hurried past, into her room.

She did not look at Dev. She picked up her shirt and put it on,
turning her back.

He laughed and she went red again.

'Cathy, I've got to go. We're working on a new album. I'll pick
you up later this evening when we're through. I've got a flat near
Sloane Square. We'll go there. You can stay there. It's a lot better
than this dump.'

'No thank you,' she said, bleakly. 'The rent's too high.'

He laughed again. 'Wait and see.'

He kissed her swiftly on the mouth. 'I swear I won't hurt you this
time.'

He went out and she heard him running down the stairs. The
front door slammed, and she watched him from the window, tall
and lithe, moving quickly up the pavement. Confident. Arrogant.
Two girls turned round and watched him. He didn't notice. He was
used to being looked at.

His big foreign car was parked on a double yellow line along the
road. He laughed up at her window and waved, and the car shot
away westwards.

She drew back. How did he know she'd be looking? Her mouth
was dry and she tried to swallow. She was shaking like a leaf now
in reaction. She sat down, hunched, on the divan.

He was *happy*. Unconcerned. It was just a minor incident to him.
He had no idea how she felt at all. He wasn't even interested, didn't
hear what she said. He knew what he wanted and he was stretching
out his hand to take it. She remembered him saying, cynically:
'Money buys everything.' He really believed that.

She noticed suddenly that the key had gone from her door. He must have taken it. Maybe he'd made a deal with the landlady too.

She stood up again, trying not to panic, desperately trying to think clearly.

After a while her brain began to function again, and turning swiftly, she pulled out her suitcase and began to pack.

Carole was pleased, but not surprised, to find Cathy back again. She said, 'I knew you'd never stick it out in that hole! We'll go out tomorrow and find something better.'

'It wasn't . . . it wasn't the place.' Cathy tried to tell her the whole story, but she found, to her horror, that she simply could not talk about it. Her mouth dried and her throat seemed to harden until she felt she could only choke. She tried several times, but the same thing happened each time. She knew that, like the taste of blood in her mouth, it was a neurotic, unhealthy, symptom, but there was nothing she could do about it.

She managed to tell Carole that she had met Paul Devlin in Nethercombe, and that he had come to her lodgings, that she hated him and couldn't bear to see him again.

For the first time since Cathy had known her, Carole seemed really impressed. Unexpectedly she laughed.

'It's frightfully romantic, Cathy. Fancy meeting one of Easy Connection by chance!'

'Oh, you don't understand!' Cathy was near to tears. 'It's not romantic. It's horrible!'

'Cathy! You can't say Paul Devlin is horrible. He's gorgeous. I've *seen* him. I was right next to the stage!' Carole was a fan and went to rock concerts with her numerous boy friends. 'Easy Connection is a fabulous band! Better than the Stones, better than Police, better than Zep. The lead singer is Chris Carter, and you never saw anything so sexy in your life!'

Cathy looked at her, interested despite herself. 'He must be different on stage. He didn't seem . . .'

'You mean you've met him, too?'

'They were both there . . . at Nethercombe.'

She remembered the bargain he had made with Dev, and

56

shivered. He must have known what Dev intended to do. He had been so kind earlier, too.

'I don't want to see *him* again either.'

Carole shook her head. 'There must be something wrong with you, Cathy. He's fantastic. Come on now, admit it.'

'Oh yes,' Cathy agreed bleakly. 'They *look* marvellous. But they're bad, Carole, really bad. I can't explain.'

'Well, you've no need to worry now. You got away. He can't find you here.'

'No, I suppose not . . .'

'You're not still worried are you, Cathy?'

'I can't seem to . . . yes.'

'But, honestly, you don't think he'll try to find you again? I mean, he can have almost anyone he wants. And you ducked out on him *twice*. Why should he bother?'

Cathy relaxed. 'No, of course he won't. I'm just being stupid. It was the shock of seeing him there in the room, when I thought I'd never see him again. I'm okay now. There's not a soul knows where I am. Even if he wanted to find me the only way would be through the College, and now I've given them my brother's address.'

'Your brother might tell him.'

'He just has the College address. I'll pick up letters from there.'

'You're all right here, anyway.'

'But I can't stay here. I've got to find a permanent place. I feel bad about coming back. But there was nowhere else I could go.'

'Don't worry, we'll find somewhere tomorrow. I'm very lucky.'

'Carole, if we find somewhere, promise you won't tell anybody my address, if they come asking . . .'

Carole was startled and offended. 'What do you take me for?'

She saw then, that tears were standing in Cathy's eyes, and that she was in an extreme state of tiredness and tension. Carole was curious. Something really bad must have happened. She had never seen Cathy like this before.

'You're all wound up like a clock spring! I promise I won't tell anybody your address. What you want now, though, is a meal, a hot drink and a long sleep. Nothing will seem so bad tomorrow!'

Cathy was grateful for Carole's mothering. Of course everything would be all right now. But as she got into bed, she had a sudden, very clear, picture of Dev, staring down at the Atlantis stone, and smiling.

Cathy's swift action had taken Dev by surprise. He was furious. The College gave her new address as the Police House, Nethercombe, and he knew that he could do nothing until the College opened. In two weeks he was starting a three-week tour of Germany and Scandinavia. It would be nearly six weeks before he saw her again, and he wanted her very badly.

He found he was holding the Atlantis stone in his fingers and he began to smile grimly. By that time she would know, and there wouldn't be any point in running away again.

# Five

The next day, Cathy and Carole took an A–Z Guide and started to explore the streets around the Art College. It was going to be even more difficult than they had thought.

The houses were large and imposing; most of them had been divided into flats for rich people. Some were offices, and some were parts of the University. Some of the smaller Regency houses were tourist hotels. Nowhere, it seemed, were there any single rooms for students. They tried the estate agents, who laughed, and some of the advertisements in the local paper, but it seemed that all accommodation was snapped up as soon as the advertisements appeared. Then they tried the newsagent's notice board, but again, everything had been taken or was too expensive.

'Well,' said Carole, near lunchtime, 'it looks like my luck ran out! Shall we have a coffee and think about what to do next? I don't think there's anything around here.' She was still cheerful.

Cathy tried not to show how tired and hopeless she felt as she trailed into the crowded snack bar after Carole.

Two men got up from a table and Cathy sat down hastily to keep a place for Carole, who went off to get the coffees. She stared out of the window, and wondered what it would be like to have a proper home. Even when her mother was alive, they had only rented the flat above a shop. If her mother had been alive now, would any of this have happened? And if her father hadn't been greedy, wanting more money than he could make in England, she might even have had a family to look after her, like other girls. Jim took after him, her mother said. Big, handsome, wanting to get on, not too bright. Insensitive and *stupid*, amended Cathy. She thought bitterly about Jim. How could he have walked away and left her in that place without noticing anything? Mary was too good for him – even if she *had* told Dev where to find her. One thing was sure, they weren't going to get her new address. They could write care of the College

She thought, if I ever make any money, the first thing I'm going to do is buy a house. Somewhere very simple and plain, but *secure* A cottage, maybe, with stone floors and whitewashed walls and hardly any furniture. No rich carpets. No marble baths. No swimming pools . . .

The boy sitting opposite glanced up casually from his book and looked again. The sun was catching Cathy's shining hair and the soft deep pink of her mouth. She glanced at him. Dark, grey-violet eyes, long dark lashes. He caught his breath, but Cathy had not noticed him. She went on staring out of the window.

'Well, we tried!' said Carole, setting down the coffee and dropping into the seat next to Cathy. 'We'll have to start looking further out.'

'Oh, Carole, what on earth am I going to do? Do you think I ought to go back to the lodgings officer and see if anything new has come in?'

Carole said, puzzled, 'You'd think there would be enough places. After all, all the students who left last July must have lived *somewhere*. What happens to those places?'

The boy had looked up from his book again. Cathy read its title upside down, *Duchamp*. Was he an art student?

She looked up and found he was staring at her. He had dark hair and eyes and a thin, intelligent face. He smiled. It transformed his rather intense, sad expression into one of amused understanding. Cathy could not resist smiling back.

'I couldn't help overhearing,' he said. 'You're looking for digs?'

'Yes. I'm starting at the London College of Art soon, but I can't get anywhere to live.'

'I'm at the London, too. Third year coming up.' They smiled at each other. He hesitated. 'There's a vacancy at our place, since Barbara moved out in July. I told the College, but they haven't sent anyone. I don't think they approve. It's mixed sharing you see. Five of us, three boys, two girls – all at the London. It's a big flat. Rather grotty. You get your own room and share the kitchen, lounge and bathroom.'

'What's the rent?' asked Cathy, holding her breath.

'A lot less than approved lodgings. But, of course, you have to get all your own food.'

60

Cathy drew a deep breath. 'Could we come and see it now?'

'Sure. It's in Hamilton Square, about ten minutes' walk. My name is Dominic Howard. Everyone calls me Nick.'

'Cathy Harlow. Carole Muir.'

They walked round the corner, and down a long road lined with Regency houses. The flat was at the far side of the Square. It was a semi-basement in a huge Edwardian block of apartments. It had its own walk-down entrance in an area, with iron railings round it. Inside it was rather dark, and everywhere looked as though it needed painting, but it had a friendly, casual atmosphere, and Cathy knew at once that she would be able to work here. There was a smell of turpentine and fried chicken.

The communal room, which everybody shared, was near the front door. It had a rush mat covering the floor, orange walls, an ancient couch, four armchairs of different shapes and colours, a table, an alcove of paperbacks and old magazines, another alcove with a home-made record deck, next to a huge opulent-looking colour television. 'On hire,' said Nick grinning. 'We share the cost.' In the window bay, uncurtained, there was a small forest of exuberant house plants of all kinds.

One wall inside the door was almost completely covered with hundreds of cut-outs – pictures, photographs, press cuttings, postcards, reproductions, quotations handwritten on scraps of paper. Some of them were brown with age. Cathy lingered, reading a *Mirror* cartoon strip, showing Bootsie being philosophical. Next to it there was a typed quotation: 'The duty of the artist is to create new ways of thought and feeling and to keep alive the human spirit.'

'You're looking at our wall? It's great for making you think.'

'I can see that. I want to stay and look at the rest. Who did it?'

'Everybody who has ever lived here over the last ten years. We never take anything down. Only add to it, if there's anything special.'

They went into the hall, with several doors leading off.

'The kitchen and the bathroom are at the end there.'

They went along a short passage. 'This would be your room.'

It was a small square room, painted white, with a divan bed, two white chests of drawers with a wide board across them to form a working desk, and three long white shelves on the wall above. There

61

was an angle lamp on the desk and another by the divan. At the end, next to a tall window, was a deep alcove with a washbasin, and a built-in cupboard with space above for cases.

The floorboards were painted glossy black, but there were no rugs, and there was nothing on the divan either.

'It looks very bare,' Nick said, grimacing, and looked at her doubtfully. 'You might like something fancier. Barbara was always trying to find somewhere better . . .'

Cathy drew breath, scarcely believing her luck.

'It's . . . marvellous! I'd really like to come if you'll have me.'

'Don't you get blankets or anything?' Carole was looking at the divan. She thought the place looked awful, but she could see that Cathy was sold on it already. At least it was near the College.

'You have to have your own bed linen and things,' said Nick, apologetically. 'But there are saucepans and china in the kitchen.'

'I've got a duvet,' said Cathy. 'But I'll need sheets and towels, and some cushions. My grant should be through soon. Maybe I can afford a rug. I've been working during the holidays.'

'What about your parents, will they mind you sharing a mixed flat? Some don't like it, you know. They think of goings-on among the artists.'

'I haven't got any parents. And I'm not interested in goings-on. I just want to get down to work. I can't wait to start at the College.'

'When do you want to move in?'

'What about the others?' Cathy said, shyly. 'Won't they want to, er, look me over first?'

'They'll be glad of anybody who'll stop them having to fork out extra rent. We don't get in each other's hair. You can be as private as you like, or as sociable. It makes no difference. There are a few rules about taking turns with general cleaning and cooking in the kitchen, but we're all very easy and relaxed. You don't look the aggressive type.' He grinned.

In fact, one of the things he had noticed about her, apart from her amazing good looks, was her control, a strange inner strength. But she was nervous – fiddling with the catch on her shoulder bag, jumping at sudden noises. He looked at her narrowly and saw she was very tense. He wondered what had happened to shake her off course.

'Can I bring my things over later today? I want to move in as soon as possible. I want to get settled and start work.'

'Suits me. But you realize I'm the only one here until next week?'

She looked at him inquiringly, then understood. She laughed, a cold, desolate little laugh, that chilled him.

'I don't have to worry,' she said. 'Tell me about the rent and extras. Do you want me to pay now?'


'Are you sure you're doing the right thing?' Carole asked doubtfully, as they went home on the bus.

'Yes,' Cathy said, without hesitation. 'It really couldn't be better. I can't believe it's true, after all the bad things recently.'

'But I know my mother wouldn't like it if she knew you were staying there with a strange boy all alone.'

Cathy laughed. 'He looked pretty normal to me. Oh, I know what you mean. But it's only for a while. I'm sure he's nice. He looked ... gentle. I don't care anyway. I've got a key to the room.'

'But ...'

'Don't you see, Carole, I don't want to be on my own in a lodging now. I mean, they'll all be back soon and if Dev did come, well, he couldn't make me ... I couldn't stand to be by myself, with another horrible landlady like that Diana.'

'And the room is so bleak!'

Cathy was surprised. 'Did you think so? I like it better when there aren't a lot of things around. It'll look fine when I get my books out, and maybe a rug. You can really work in a plain white room.'

Carole laughed affectionately. 'You'd be happy in a nun's cell.'

Cathy said lightly, 'I would, but they wouldn't have me now.' To her horror, Carole saw that Cathy was crying.

She put her arm round her and hugged her.

'Stop it, Cathy! You mustn't keep crying. I think you ought to come with me to the doctor.'

But Cathy refused, almost hysterically. She said she was just tired and worried, but if she could get her things back to Hamilton Square, she could feel settled and relaxed. Privately she knew that she was near the end of her control. Too much had happened too quickly in the last few days. Too much emotion. She needed desperately to be by herself, to sleep for a long time.

She made a last effort. Got her cases repacked, went shopping in the local shops for extra groceries and other essentials, and with a mini-cab and Carole's help moved everything over to Hamilton Square.

After Carole had gone, promising to ring her before she went off to her teaching college, Cathy sat on her newly made up divan, hardly able to believe that she was truly in her own place at last. The kind of place she had always wanted. Carole's mother had given her some perfectly good sheets which she said she no longer needed, and Carole had given her a huge fluffy towel as a moving-in present. Cathy had nearly burst into tears again.

She unpacked her things and, taking the big bag of groceries, went in search of Nick.

He showed her which cupboard in the kitchen was hers, and she packed everything away. She said, trying to smile. 'I've been a bit worried, lately. All the moving round, and not having anywhere to live ... other things, too. I'm a bit ... tense. If you don't see me around for a while, I'll be sleeping.'

He could see the grey veil of fatigue drawn over her features, dark shadows under her eyes.

He smiled back, gently. 'Thanks for telling me. Don't worry about a thing. Sleep all you want. Nobody will disturb you. You'll be quite safe here.' He never knew why he said that, but he saw the tears come into her eyes before she turned hastily away.

She slept properly, for the first time since Saturday. By the end of the week she began to feel almost normal, and some of her energy and optimism had begun to return. She had slept deeply, waking dazed, sitting quietly looking through her sketches, not thinking much, then sleeping again. She ate when she felt like it, then slept again.

Nick came and went so quietly, she hardly heard him, and then, towards the end of the week, he came into the kitchen, where she was heating a tin of soup.

She smiled at him. 'Hello! Do you want some soup?'

'Is there enough?'

He came over and took her face in his hands and turned it to the light. She had washed her hair and it shone smooth and gold. The shadow strain had gone from her eyes and her skin had lost the unhealthy pale blue pallor. She was very beautiful. 'You're better.'

The colour came into her cheeks. She laughed. 'Much better! I've come out of the tunnel and everything's new. I can't wait to get started. I've so many ideas, they're bursting out of me.'

Several times after that they shared meals in the kitchen. They talked, and he began to be real for her. Until then, he had been a shadowy figure, with a pleasant face, but now she began to realize what a very nice person he was. *Gentle*, she thought, that was the clue to his character. She could not imagine him ever doing anything to hurt anyone.

'Are you going to show me your work?' he asked, one day.

'I haven't got much here, and I'm sort of shy about it because it's not what I want. I don't know *how* to do what I want to do yet.'

'What are you interested in?'

'People. I want to . . . get down inside their minds. To show what they are, how they think.'

'Portraits?'

'Not exactly. That's not enough. I want to show people in their *places*, their rooms, houses, factories, in the spaces around them. We didn't have a chance to do much figure drawing in my school, and although I did a course at the local college, I've got a lot of work to do before I can even begin to paint what I want.'

He looked at her doubtfully. 'Sometimes you can do too many studies. Be technically too good. It can knock out the intuition, the direct knowledge that comes as you work. Do you get me?'

'Not very well.'

'I'm thinking of the painter Kokoschka, with his head wound from the war, painting portraits of people *as they were going to be* a few years later. You couldn't do studies for that kind of thing. The knowledge comes from . . . well, somewhere else.'

'You think perhaps I ought to start straight in on the painting? Not wait until I've developed a better drawing technique? I don't think I've got enough confidence yet.'

He shrugged. 'How am I to know? I was just warning you about putting all your trust in technique.'

'Have a look at my drawings, and tell me what you think.'

She fetched her portfolio, and spread it open, avoiding his eyes.

She felt shy and terribly nervous. It was the first time anyone outside school had looked at her work.

He went through the drawings, pausing here and there, looking back occasionally, not saying anything at all. Then he closed the folder, tied the strings and looked at her enigmatically.

'You did these at the college?'

'The figure studies. The flowers and interiors at school. The landscapes –' she looked away – 'at my brother's recently. What do you think? Are they all right?'

'You already draw better than I do. Better than most of us at College.' His voice was even, stating a fact.

She stared, astonished. 'I don't believe you!'

He shrugged and laughed at her expression.

'But they never said anything at school. Just that I was good, and that I ought to go to art school.'

'Didn't want you to get a big head!' He laughed again. He could not tell her yet that he was staggered at the quality of her drawing, at the intense observation, the *skill*.

'I think you're being kind. I just haven't done enough figure drawing. I'm dying to get started.'

'You'll see. I should think you're a cert for the Gold Medal this year. Come and see my work now.'

His room was slightly larger than her own, lighter and emptier, dominated by three large canvases, two metres by three metres. She sat down on his divan and looked at them carefully.

Despite what he had said about his drawing she could see that these canvases had been drawn out meticulously. They must be the end product of many previous studies, and she saw piled in the corner a large number of watercolour studies. The paintings were severely abstract, with thin delicate vertical lines crossed by equally delicate horizontal lines, barely visible on the brilliant white canvas. And then, as she looked longer, she was suddenly aware of a rainbow iridescence, criss-crossing the whole area, a network of glinting colour, like a cobweb with dew on it on a sunlit morning.

She looked from one to the other, in that deep almost trance-like concentration he had begun to recognize. At last she looked at him. 'I wish I had the money to buy one. They're so beautiful.' He could hear the excitement, respect, in her voice.

66

He looked embarrassed. 'Thanks.'

'They must have taken forever to plan out. And paint.'

'Those three took nearly all last year. There was a set theme for work – "Sunlight on Surfaces". They came out of all that stuff in the corner.'

'Is that what they do then? Make a set theme?'

'Sometimes. You'll probably get that in your first year anyway. Several set themes. But they are very open – plenty of space for your own ideas.'

'Are you doing this kind of work for your Degree Show?'

He nodded. 'That pile over *there* is the preliminary work. I'm looking at sunlight on water now, and rain, falling on shining surfaces like glass and chrome.' He sighed. 'It's hard looking, I can tell you. I like working out the colour changes, but it's donkey work to paint.'

She laughed. 'Hard painting makes good looking!'

He laughed too. 'I'm just starting to rule up the next canvas.' She saw it, half-hidden behind one of the other pictures. The fine pencil lines were meticulously measured, with no errors, so fine they could barely be seen.

'And you said I was good at drawing!'

He said seriously, 'I couldn't draw the way you do. Seeing all the details so clearly, putting it down so ... accurately, with – I don't know how to explain – your drawings are like those extra special dreams, with everything glowing. Do you take anything?'

She was puzzled. 'Take anything?'

'Acid. Snow.'

'No!' She was indignant. 'If I screw my mind up like that, how will I see what's there?'

'Sorry, but they seemed so – visionary.'

'Is that why you looked at me so peculiarly when you closed up my folder?' She began to laugh.

'No. I was thinking that in a few years I'd be boasting I was at College with Catherine Harlow.'

She laughed, but he did not join in, and she wondered, briefly, if he could be serious.

Cathy was sleeping normally now. She felt so good and relaxed that she was able to settle into her room properly. She cleaned it thoroughly, polishing until everything shone. She arranged her books on the shelves, and in the local street market, she found a scarlet cotton washable rug, and a length of plain scarlet cotton fabric to go with it, which she hemmed into a bedcover. She splashed out and bought two large cushions which could be used on the divan or on the floor, and she covered these in another cheap length of fabric from the market, navy blue with huge scarlet daisy flowers with white centres.

She looked round the room with satisfaction. It was still plain, but the red glowed against the white walls, and the dark shining floor and the cushions looked very smart. She began to paint a little portrait of Carole, for Carole's mother, as a thank-you present.

London was basking in a beautiful Indian summer, and she went swimming with Nick in the park, each day, and got a light tan sunbathing in the hot sun. They went to a complicated foreign film, full of angled shots and strange colour.

She did not try to hide from herself that good, gentle Nick was having a great deal to do with her recovery.


The College was reopening and the flat's other occupants began to drift back, one at a time.

Julie Ellis, starting her third year in fashion design, came on Thursday. Cathy was nervous of meeting her, hoping she would not be too superior and glossy. She was neither. She was small, brown-haired, with a sweet smile.

'Oh, am I pleased to see you!' she exclaimed, laughing, and hugging Cathy. 'My father said if they didn't get another girl I would have to move! Haven't you made it nice in here ... Oh, *where* did you get that navy and red daisy fabric? It's just what I want for the beachwear outfit I'm doing ...'

'In the market. It was quite cheap.'

'Will you show me? Oh, I think this year is going to be *fun*. I'm sure we're going to get on. Between you and me, I wasn't awfully keen on Barbara, who was here. She was – well, very dissatisfied and bitchy and she led poor old Nick a dog's life. He was terribly in love with her, you know. And she was so *cruel* ... Oh!' She clapped a hand over her mouth, her brown eyes exasperated. 'There I go *again*. I'm just a big blabber-mouth. I'd better go.'

Cathy couldn't help laughing. 'It's all right. I guessed anyway – from things Nick said.'

Julie looked at her critically. 'He'll tell you I expect. It'd be a good thing if you caught him on the rebound. You look as though you'd be good for him.'

Cathy laughed. 'What about you?'

'Oh, I'm engaged already. No, I don't wear a ring. It's not official yet, but I've known him all my life. He's studying too. Accountancy. And when we finish next year we plan to set up in business. You'll meet him soon. He comes here quite often, although he's going off to Cambridge on a course soon. We have a lot of visitors. People are always dropping in. Now I must go and unpack. Don't forget, tomorrow we're going down the market.'

Bernard Brown came on Saturday, very tall and broad, with shaggy, unkempt hair, and huge hands. He came in riotously, shouting out to Nick, kissing Julie with a loud smack, and catching Cathy round her waist he lifted her effortlessly off the floor and looked at her with surprised satisfaction.

'Hey, we got a fairy lady!' He gave her a smacking kiss, too. 'Start as you mean to go on, I always say.'

'You can just put the fairy lady down,' said Nick. 'She isn't used to rough, uncouth sculptors.'

'So?' Bernard's bright blue eyes gleamed inquiringly at her. 'Aaarrgh! Don't tell me. *Too late again!*' He staggered, clowning, round the kitchen, clutching his heart and head, then reverted startlingly to normal.

'You did better this time, man. Thank God Barbara's gone.'

Cathy realized that Bernard had assumed that she was Nick's new girl. She waited for him to explain, but he said nothing.

'Why did you let him think I'm your girl?' she said, curiously, when they were alone.

He grinned. 'Bernard's a wolf in wolf's clothing. Let him find out for himself. I'm not giving any help to the opposition. Why, do you fancy him?'

She blushed. 'No. I just wondered.'

Last to arrive on Sunday evening was Alun Owen, another painter. He was small, dark hair, dark eyes, rather drunk, singing a temperance hymn in a fine tenor voice and clutching a large bottle.

69

'Torn himself from the embraces of the delicious Myfanwy at last,' said Bernard.

'Hello, Alun. Still playing the stage Welshman?' said Nick.

'Ah, boyo, you don't understand the singing soul of the Welsh. We *feel*, we *talk*, we scale the heights, feel passion, despair ...' Still talking he swooped about the room, miraculously assembling glasses to pour the wine.

'Shut up, Alun,' said Julie. 'Look, here's Cathy, our new flat mate.'

His dark eyes surveyed her like an X-ray. 'Aah!' he said, reverently, at last. 'Straight out of the mists of legend ... Briar Rose, Beggar Maid ... Yseult ... Mariana ... Millais, Burne-Jones, boys, you missed your finest hour!'

Cathy, confused, looked at Nick.

'He thinks you look like a Pre-Raphaelite girl,' he translated.

Cathy went red.

'Look, she even blushes, too. But can she cook better than bloody Barbara?'

'Alun, you drunken, lazy, chauvinist pig,' said Julie, indignantly. 'She's got her work to do. She's not going to spend all her time cooking for you lot.'

All three boys immediately howled despairingly.

Julie said to Cathy, 'Alun's quite a good cook, don't let him have you on.'

Cathy laughed. 'I don't mind taking a turn cooking Sunday dinner now and again. I can't do fancy things though.'

'Yorkshire Pudding?'

'If you like.'

'Roast potatoes?'

'Roast potatoes.'

'Apple pie?'

'*Frozen* apple pie.'

'I don't believe it,' said Bernard. 'Girls who look like you can't cook.'

'I only do ordinary things.'

'Nick,' said Alun, turning to him respectfully. 'If, last term, I ever said anything to lead you to suppose I thought you a half-witted idiot ...'

'You said, quote, there's so many holes in your head it's like a Victorian lace curtain, unquote. You said, quote, your brain is as soft as pigswill, unquote, You said . . .'

'I take it all back. You are a genius. *A genius*. You shall have another glass of wine for finding Cathy. Here – let's have a suitable toast to the new term. Yorkshire Pudding!'

They drank, laughing, and Cathy suddenly realized she was as happy as she had ever been in her life.

Keeping her address a secret had worked. There was no sign of Dev. She had shaken him off permanently. Carole was right – he wasn't going to bother.

# Six

The College opened, and soon a routine was established. Other new students found difficulty in settling in, but Cathy began to work immediately, with the intense concentration which was characteristic of her. At last she felt she was doing what she was meant to do, after all the long years of waiting. She went in an hour earlier than most other students and hardly ever left the building until the caretaker came round to lock up just after nine. She had a meal, and then worked again, in her room, sometimes late into the night. Occasionally she shared a pot of tea with Nick who also liked to paint late at night.

She was working on the set theme, 'Distortion', in three areas – painting, the metal workshop and the glass studio. The studies, ideas, experiments came so fast she could not find time to do them all. She began to worry about her grant money holding out for materials. On Sundays she wandered through the empty back streets of the City of London, drawing the reflections of reflections of windows in the great office blocks, or went with Nick to stand for hours on the Embankment, watching the shadows breaking and fraying in the water under Waterloo Bridge.

She found a stall in the market which sold old spectacle lenses. Held against a mirror they produced strange optical illusions and distortions of the objects in the room. She was not quite sure what to do with them, but she knew somehow that it was related to what she wanted to do in her figure paintings. She made drawing after drawing of the illusions.

But of all the things she was doing, it was her life drawing which gave her the greatest delight and the greatest agony.

She could *see* so clearly what needed to be done, but no matter how hard she worked, still the figures would not come as she wanted.

72

'They ought to kind of *flow* on to the paper, effortlessly, as though they had always been there,' she said to Nick, in desperation. 'You know what I mean?'

'I know what you mean, but I don't know why you're worrying. You're better than all of us already. I heard Bob Crossley talking to Ziggard on Thursday about your life drawing. They're really impressed, Cathy.'

She smiled. 'Well, I suppose that's nice to know. But not much use, when *I* know I'm not getting it down right. Like those Japanese and Chinese drawings.'

'Well, of course, a lot of those artists were Buddhists. They meditated for days, sometimes, before they started the drawing.'

'Meditated?'

'Oh, you know. You sit quietly, relax and sort of sink deep into your mind, not worrying, not thinking of anything. You can concentrate on your breathing, or on repeating one word over and over again, or on the thing you're going to draw. Then, when you're ready you start. Just letting your mind work through your hand. You have to stop *trying*.'

She looked at him. 'You've done it?'

'I did some TM, that's Transcendental Meditation, a couple of years ago. It works, but it seems slow. It's not intellectual enough for me. I like to work things out with my mind.'

'How long do you have to meditate?'

'It varies. At least twenty minutes.'

'I'll try it. Just as soon as the conditions are right. I couldn't do it in the life room, with Bob Crossley prowling around behind me. The poses are only ten or twenty minutes usually.'

It was difficult, she found, to get models. If she just sat and looked at people, they grew restless and uncomfortable, and moved away before she got to the drawing part. She tried the method using a potted geranium instead, and was astonished at the free, expressive result. Now, if only she could work out some way she could do people – people who went on doing whatever it was they were doing and didn't mind being stared at. In the meantime, she persevered with the traditional method, trying to loosen up, working in a relaxed way, letting her intuition take over, and was much more pleased with the results.

At Hamilton Square, the sharing arrangement was very success-
ful. She got on well with everyone, cooking the occasional meal for
them when they all got together with a bottle of wine. But there was
no question of her spending a lot of time cooking, as Julie had feared.
She simply was not there. She was working.

Nick was disappointed. 'You work too hard. I hardly ever see
you.'

'You can't work too hard. Not when it's pleasure. It's so marvellous to be doing art all the time. I even enjoy the history of art
lectures.'

The thing that pleased her most of all was that there were always
other people about when she felt sociable. She had always been
something of a loner – her brother was so much older, her mother
always at work, and at school most of the girls her own age seemed
only interested in clothes and boys, and couldn't understand her
obsessive need to paint and draw. It was marvellous to know that
she had only to go into the kitchen or the lounge to find some
interesting talk going on.

She found that their flat was the meeting place of a much wider
group in the College. In every year there are students who stand out
by reason of their abilities or personalities, and most of these found
their way to Hamilton Square. They discussed everything under the
sun – ideas, politics, sex, sport and art, art, art. Often she felt she
was understanding what she thought about things for the first time.
There was a marvellous atmosphere of fun and freedom.

She realized how lucky she had been to find such a place, and
make such good friends. London could be terribly lonely.

The episode with Dev seemed so far away – like a bad nightmare
– and she hardly thought of it at all now.

She knew it was Nick who had helped her most of all. He had
shown her that some men were good and kind, and not to be feared.
He was gentle always, and seemed to have time to help everybody.

They had similar tastes, and their opinions on most subjects
agreed. Sometimes they seemed so mentally in tune that it startled
her. It was a very loving and relaxed friendship. No strains. No
hassles. But it was not just a friendship. Although they had not
spoken of it, they were beginning to be in love with each other. He
kissed her, but there had been . . . something. He didn't know what.

74

Perhaps it was the way she had turned away, a little too quickly, and for a brief moment he had seen the strain back on her face.

'What is it?'

She swallowed. 'Nothing. It'll be all right. Give it a little time. Don't let's spoil things.'

He was content to leave it like that for the time being. He didn't want to get too deeply involved again, distracted from his work, with the Degree Show looming over him at the end of the year. But their loving, undemanding friendship settled him and concentrated his mind, helping him to recover from the hurt of his love affair with Barbara. There was no hurry. Their loving was coming into bloom, slowly, growing in gentleness.

He told her about Barbara, and she held his hand tightly and wished she could tell him about Cox's Farm, but she still could not talk about it. She could not tell him yet how unclean she was. One day she would tell him and he would understand, and would help her, but not yet. She only wanted to forget and work.

He told her too, about his family and home in Hertfordshire, and she found he had a passion for rock music. 'Hard rock,' he said, 'not this muck in the top ten.'

He played guitar and organ, and had had a difficult choice between art and music.

He smiled. 'We had this group at school. I wanted desperately to be a rock star. I suppose most boys do.' He smiled again, shame-faced. 'Perhaps I still do.'

'Why didn't you try?'

'Temperament. Personality. They wouldn't fit. I could play, all right. But can you see *me* dominating an audience of forty thousand, like the Stones, Easy Connection?'

The name jolted her. She remembered the vivid, larger-than-life quality of Dev, as she had last seen him from the window, supremely confident, assured. She remembered Dev and Chris sprawled exhausted on the sofa, and yet their physical magnetism, the aura of personality, dominating the room. She had felt it even before she knew who they were.

She got up restlessly and went to the window so that he should not see her face.

'It's not a real life.'

'No, not real. Super-real. You create your life like a work of art if you're a rock musician. It's not just the music. *You* are a work of art yourself. I suppose that's what attracted me. The idea of making a total creation. You *and* your work.'

'You can do that as a painter,' she said dubiously, interested despite herself. 'Plenty of people have.'

He ran a hand through his hair. 'Maybe it was just the attraction of opposites. You always want to be the opposite of what you are. You know, wild extroverts want to be austere intellectuals ... Anyway, it's too late now. I'm committed. I enjoy my work here. I think I'm fairly good. If I'd gone in for rock I'd be wishing I did painting. Rock takes up about twenty per cent of my time now.'

'You still play?'

'There's a band here in College.'

'I'm glad you didn't become a rock star. That kind of life – it destroys you. All that money and power and fan worship. Big houses. Luxury. It kills everything real. Even their feelings ... They get hard and cruel and arrogant ...'

He was staring at her curiously. 'You know somebody in the business?'

She had nearly given herself away. 'Th-that's how it seems to me.'

'I don't think it's as bad as you say,' he said slowly. 'I go to a lot of clubs, concerts, and the guys are just ordinary musicians. Very into their music. I know there's a lot of hype but the music is real.'

He smiled at her. 'You like jazz. I'll come to Ronnie Scott's with you, if you'll come to rock clubs with me. Right?'

She hesitated. She need not go to any Easy Connection concerts after all, and the sort of clubs Nick would go to would be the places students went. Anyway, Dev would have forgotten all about her by now.

'All right,' she said, stretching out her hand and laughing. 'It's a deal. But don't expect too much of me. I don't know about rock.'

So he took her to his favourite venues, mostly small, student places, and she listened and watched unknown bands who might one day make it big, if they stayed together long enough.

Listening to the groups she began to enjoy rock music and to respect the skill of some of the musicians who played it.

Best of all, she discovered she had solved her problem of finding models who did not object to being just stared at.

Nobody objected to her staring at the lead singer, or the bass guitarist, or whatever, for twenty minutes. They were just what she wanted for her meditation-type drawings. They moved, turned, twisted, threw their arms and legs about into extreme positions. She could go into the deepest trance, then bring out her sketchbook unobtrusively, and draw them with that flowing expressive line. It could not be better!

They began to go to the clubs more frequently. The improvement in her drawing delighted her. She felt she might even be ready to start painting the kind of pictures she dreamed about. She had once thought it would be years before she was ready, but after only a few weeks . . .

No, it was longer than that. But there had been so much happening, so much work and talk and fun and enjoyment, the time had just sped away.

She looked in her diary and added up the weeks. Surely it couldn't be *that* long! Nearly two months since she had come to Hamilton Square. Her mind blocked and a wave of panic spread through her. She looked at the marked red dates and added up the days again, but there was no mistake.

She went into the kitchen and drank a glass of water, shakily. It couldn't be anything serious. All the excitement and upset . . . It had happened before . . . *Twice?* Well, maybe she would check with the doctor sometime. But now she must really get down to work. The paintings must be started immediately.

# Seven

'They're good for a support group.'

'They're always good here.'

Cathy and Nick were sitting in Azra's, one of their favourite music places. It had started as a very cheap, natural food café, and the students had colonized it. After a while, the owner had started to invite up-and-coming groups to play in the cellar. Now it was becoming an 'in' place for trendy people, and the prices had risen accordingly.

'We won't be able to afford it much longer,' said Nick, gloomily. 'They're even reserving tables now!' He poked his finger disgustedly at the next table which had its chairs tipped forward.

They were there for a special treat, because he thought she was working a lot too hard. For the last couple of weeks she had been even quieter than usual, working through the night, hardly stopping for meals, driving herself on at a dangerous rate. Several times he had seen the old strained look back. There was something wrong, he was sure. But she kept saying that she was all right, and that she must get on with her work. Even tonight she had insisted upon bringing her sketchbook.

He said, looking round, 'There's a lot of well-known people here. A lot of musicians. There's Jay Bird of the Bird Lovers. It must be the band.'

'This one?'

'No, the one we've come for. Night Mission. You must have heard of them. Even you will be impressed. No gimmicks. All solid musicianship. Two of them were Royal College of Music people. They've been touring the States during the summer. Had a couple of things in the charts earlier in the year, but they are much better than that. They're heading for the top. They write their own stuff and it's really good – original.'

78

A lot of other people obviously thought so too, because the Club began to fill up quickly, and when Night Mission took the stand and began to play, Cathy could understand why.

They played with a fierce savagery that she had not come across before. There was a powerful, tall, bass player, a black drummer, one of the best she had ever heard, and two outstanding guitarists. One with smooth gold hair, and an intelligent, amused face, wearing dark glasses and the other, dark-haired, with powerful shoulders, arrogant and exciting, with a personal magnetism that riveted all the female eyes in the Club. A virtuoso, she thought. Quite simply the best electric guitarist she had heard so far. As good as Eric Clapton, Jimmy Page, Paul Devlin. He did the singing too, in a rough, throaty, blues voice.

By the end of their third number, she had stopped drawing and was looking with astonishment at Nick. He grinned at her.

'Told you so!'

'Who is he?'

'Dave Hampton.'

'Why are they playing *here*? I would have thought –'

'Old times' sake, I should think. They were here a lot before they made it big.'

There was a driving excitement about their playing which built up and built up, feeding on the rising response of the audience. Soon everybody, including the band itself, began to realize it was going to be no ordinary evening. It was one of those special times which afterwards become legendary. 'Do you remember the night the Mission played Azra's?' people would say, years later.

They played for an hour and brought their first set to an end with *Jump off the Top*, a heaving, screaming, whirlwind of sound, which had the audience, including Cathy and Nick, on its feet, cheering and clapping.

She was so absorbed in the band that she did not immediately notice the eddying movement of the crowd near the door, the people turning round and moving apart to let them through, almost like royalty.

Azra himself came past. 'Over here, I kept a table for you ...' And then Nick, excited, exclaimed in her ear: 'Wow! Will you look at this? Easy Connection! I've never seen them here before!'

The room swung sickeningly about her, but she managed to tu[rn] her head away and slide out of sight behind Nick as Dev and Chr[is] with two men and two girls, came through the heavy cigare[tte] smoke.

She sat down hastily. She must not, *could* not, faint here. S[he] must not panic. They hadn't see her, and after all this time D[ev] wouldn't remember her. He must have forgotten all about [it] now.

She heard Nick saying, 'That's Chris Carter and Paul Devlin, ar[d] the drummer, Keith Hurst. I think the plump man with th[e] moustache must be their manager, Bill Hopkins.'

They were laughing, and looked high on drink or something els[e]. They were assured, confident. Not showing off, but well aware [of] the excitement and sensation they were causing.

She had forgotten how beautiful they were.

They sat down, joking, waving to friends at other tables, and the[n] Dave Hampton came over and joined them for a drink, smiling f[or] the first time that evening. Cathy saw, from the way they said hell[o] that he must be a special friend. Dev lifted his head to glance roun[d] arrogantly, almost as though he knew he was under speci[al] scrutiny, then he flung back his head and laughed at somethin[g] Chris had said, and Cathy's heart lurched as she recognized the not[e] of wild, reckless desperation that had been there at Cox's Farm.

She slid further down in her seat, her hands shaking. Now wa[s] the time to go, while they were talking together. They were makin[g] a lot of noise and wouldn't notice if people left. When the musi[c] started again it would be impossible.

She tried to draw her courage around her and stop the tremblin[g] of her legs and arms.

'I . . . I think I'd like to go, Nick.'

He turned to look at her gaping in astonishment. '*Go!* But *Cathy* we've heard only half the . . .'

His voice rose, louder than usual, coinciding with a moment o[f] silence at the next table. Cathy saw, with supernatural clarity an[d] anguish, both Dev and Chris freeze, and look round together.

She turned quickly and pressed her face into Nick's shoulder. H[e] put his arm round her. 'Cathy,' he was whispering, his head ben[t] over her, 'Do you mean . . . ?'

But it was too late. She heard a chair go over, and the next instant ѐr hands had been seized and she was pulled to her feet.

'*Cathy!* Sweet little baby!'

She was swept off her feet into the air and swung round between ѡe tables. Dev's laughter was wild, almost hysterical, but suddenly broke and he pulled her hard against him and kissed her deeply ѧn the mouth.

Darkness whirled, and then she heard the whistles and the ѧughter from the crowded room. She pulled her mouth free, but he ̓ould not let her go. He kissed the hollow of her neck, and then ѡolding her head so she could not move, he began kissing her again, ̓ke a thirsty man finding water in a desert.

'Don't, Dev! Please! Everybody's looking!' She was breathless, ̓carlet, almost in tears.

'What about it? Let them look. They can see you belong to me.' Ѕis voice carried clear across the room.

'*No.* Let me go!' She caught a glimpse of his manager's face, ̭oking worried.

Dev kept his arm round her. 'Oh, *hell*, Cathy! Where have you ѥen? I've had two roadies and a private dick looking for you for ѡeeks, since we got back from Sweden. I thought you'd gone for ̩ood, you silly little bitch!'

He made no attempt to keep his voice down. He was used to living ѡis life in the full gaze of the public, and it didn't matter to him any ѣore. Cathy felt she would like to sink through the floor. Everyone ̭as staring and listening avidly. They had thought it was a joke – ̩he famous star giving a pretty girl a kiss, but now they knew it was ѣore than a joke. Another Easy Connection scandal. He had made ̩t sound as though she had been living with him. *What must Nick ѥ thinking?* Her heart wrenched.

She stood away from Dev, paper white, and tried to speak ѣormally.

'I just ... changed my lodgings. I didn't know you were looking ̓or me.'

He stared at her. His eyes moved slowly over her body and came ̍back to her face. 'I reckon you ought to be looking for *me*.'

She tried to hold that gleaming, penetrating gaze, but the colour flooded brilliantly under her skin, burning darker. Tell-tale.

81

'So!' He was laughing loudly, exultantly. He caught her to h▮ and kissed her again.

She was suddenly, furiously angry, not scared. How dare ▮ laugh. How dare he kiss her like this – *like a possession*!

'Let me go!' She struggled out of his clasp. 'Why should I look f▮ you? I don't need you!'

He stared at her dangerously for a second, then he looked direct▮ at Nick.

'Who's he?'

She put out her hand and Nick came and stood next to her. Sh▮ slipped her hand into his, and he felt her fingers shaking.

'This is my friend, Nick Howard, from College.'

Dev's eyes took in their interlinked fingers, went to their face▮ and understood. His eyes went black. His hands curled in▮ fists.

His manager got up hastily, pushing between them.

'For God's sake, Dev, remember where you are. What are yo▮ trying to do to the girl?' His low, furious voice had an effect, an▮ Dev turned away, looking murderous.

'I'm Bill Hopkins, Dev's manager. You'd better sit down.' It wa▮ an order, not a request. His voice was hostile. He began turning th▮ chairs around.

'No,' said Cathy, clearly. 'We're just leaving.'

'Oh no, you're not!' said Dev, and putting his arm round her lik▮ a vice, he propelled her to the next table. 'I want to introduce yo▮ to my friends.'

'You've met Bill already. The girl I don't know. Chris picked he▮ up some place last night and she's hanging on . . .'

Cathy realized he was much drunker than he seemed, and much more dangerous.

'This is Keith Hurst, our drummer.'

He was tall, very thin, very dark, with deep-set eyes that knew pain. She remembered that Chris had said he had taken a year t▮ kick heroin addiction. He smiled and his face changed from a▮ brooding darkness to amused charm.

'Welcome to the band, Cathy Harlow.' It was an odd greeting. Sh▮ wondered how he knew her name.

'Lisa, Keith's wife.' The other girl, pretty, heavily pregnant,

82

_iled_ at Cathy and winked sympathetically. 'Sit down, love, _ey're_ a bit overwhelming. You'll get used to them.'

'That's right!' said Dev. 'Sit down and talk to Lisa, you've got a _t_ in common.' He laughed.

'Hello, Cathy,' said Chris. He was lounging back, next to Lisa, _miling._

She met his eyes, briefly. Her colour rose. He had known what _ev_ intended that night and did nothing to help her. He had handed _er_ over to Dev.

She nodded, unsmiling. 'Chris.'

'No smile for me, Cathy?'

She shook her head dumbly.

'For the bullocks?'

Her eyes were dark, accusing.

He looked at her. 'Don't blame me, Cathy. That way I thought _d_ get you too. Anything wrong in that?'

She drew a shocked breath. They were outrageous. There was _nothing_ they wouldn't do or say, no matter who was listening. She _lanced_ quickly at Dev, but he was laughing. Her eyes, defenceless, _net_ Dave Hampton's. He looked at her with interest and smiled.

'That's Dave Hampton you're looking at,' said Dev. 'One of the _est_ guitar players in the business.'

'I know,' she said, suddenly smiling back at Dave, remembering _her_ pleasure. 'I just heard him.'

'That's right, I forgot,' said Dev, mocking, savage. 'She doesn't _ike_ rock, but she can tell you all about your jazz influences. Go on, _sweetie,_ give Dave a reading. Tell him who he's been listening to.'

'Please, I don't want . . .'

Chris said, 'She likes him, Dev. She smiled at _him_.'

'Yeah, I noticed.'

'But she couldn't tell they were bullocks, Dev.'

'She likes his eyes, Chris.'

They laughed. 'Go on, sweetie, do your party piece. You wouldn't want to disappoint Dave, would you?'

The cat and mouse act. They were punishing her. For smiling at Dave? No, of course, there was more. She had run away, twice. Dev wanted to hurt her because he understood about Nick, and Chris . . . she did not know why Chris wanted to hurt her.

83

'Our baby's not going to be good, Dev. She's not going to do it.'

'She doesn't like doing it in front of strangers, Chris.'

They laughed again, watching her narrowly.

It was then she realized that it wasn't just a game to hurt – the were demonstrating to everybody their knowledge of her, the *ownership* of her.

The whole room seemed to be looking at her. She drew in a ragge breath. She must get it over with, and get away, *quickly*. She swa lowed and said, huskily, 'Howlin' Wolf? Broonzy. Big Bill Broonz And ...' She swallowed again. 'Do you play classical guitar?' F nodded. 'Then it's Segovia, and maybe Julian Bream a bit.'

Dave laughed. 'Right! That's clever.'

'Our baby *is* clever!' said Chris, approvingly.

'But naughty, sometimes, Dave. Thinks she knows better than w do.'

Cathy glanced at Nick. He was looking from Chris to Dev fascinated, and then at her, as though he was seeing her for the fir: time. She shivered and moved close to him, clutching his han tightly for support.

'Please let's go now, Nick.'

Keith Hurst was laughing aloud, his head thrown back.

'For God's sake, Chris, don't tell me you're sharing her! I though she was Dev's girl.'

'That's right,' said Dev. 'We're getting married.'

Then, seeing her expression, he began laughing recklessly.

'My fi ... arnnnnn ... saaay!' The drawled, perfect, Souther: States accent, ludicrously coy, sent the surrounding tables int guffaws of laughter. Dev, hearing, immediately swung around, hi eyes alight. He bowed to the crowded room. 'Ladies and gentlemen Catherine Harlow, my fi ... arnnn ... saaay!' He sounded as thougl he was making an announcement at Wembley.

Everywhere people were laughing indulgently or excitedly, wait ing for some more Easy Connection histrionics, and some people entering into the spirit, started clapping. 'Take a bow, Cathy ...'

Cathy's mouth was dry with fear. In their terrible mood she knew he was capable of anything. This is how he had been that day .. She kept her eyes on his manager, and tried not to think of all the listeners.

'It's not true,' she said. 'He's joking.'

'No more jokes, Cathy,' said Dev, savagely, his mood swinging. 'All the jokes are over now. Even that bastard there, holding your hand and the two of you looking like love's young dream – that joke is over too!'

She felt Nick's hand tighten convulsively.

'No!'

'Oh yes it is. And you know why, too.'

Nick detached his hand and moved forward. 'I don't like the way you're talking to her.'

Dev was surprised and amused. He looked Nick over more carefully, taking in his age, his build, his gentleness. Then, unforgivably, he laughed, almost kindly.

'Move along, boy. You're outclassed.'

'Don't call me boy!' Nick began to lose his temper.

Dave Hampton got up from the table, seemingly unhurried, and yet he was there, like a wall between them.

'Well, all this is very interesting, but I've got to go do a set. I came over to ask if you'd care to do a little jamming with us, Dev, but I guess it's not the right time.'

He smiled down at Cathy, and she knew it was not true. He had not come to ask Dev to play. He was creating a diversion to allow her to get away, or maybe to stop his friend Dev getting into a fight.

Dev looked at him, tempted. 'And have baby here running off again as soon as my back is turned?'

Nick said evenly. 'We're not running anywhere. We came to hear Night Mission. We're staying until the end.'

Dev smiled at her mockingly. 'That true, Cathy?'

She looked miserably at the table. She couldn't wait to get out of the place. How could she endure another hour of this, with everybody staring at her?

'I suppose so.'

He stood looking at her for a moment. Then he laughed, his mood changing. 'Come on then, let's see if I can borrow a guitar.'

'There's a Fender Strat at the back, or you can have my Gibson.'

'The Strat will do.' They went off together.

'Well?' said Bill Hopkins, angrily.

'W-well what?'

'Are you marrying him? I've got to know, unless you want to be ripped apart by the media tomorrow morning.'

'The newspapers!' Cathy was horrified.

'Newspapers, television, radio, magazines, the lot.'

'But how will they know? What's it got to do with them?'

Everybody at the table, except Nick, laughed.

'You don't think Paul Devlin of Easy Connection can get married without the papers being interested do you? What am I supposed to say?'

'Of course I'm not marrying him! He's *drunk*.' She was disgusted.

Bill Hopkins shrugged wearily. 'So what's new? He's been drunk more or less since we came back from Sweden.'

'What's the matter with him now?'

'You,' said Chris. 'He hasn't seen you for two months. He thought he'd know where you were when we got back. But they haven't been able to find you at the College, and they couldn't get an address out of your friend Carole.'

'You haven't been bothering Carole!'

Bill Hopkins grunted. 'Not me, sweetheart. Lover boy. You're just a damned nuisance to me.'

She was red and angry. 'I hardly know him. He's not my lover.'

'Don't tell me, sweetheart. Tell him. Only, for Chrissakes *not tonight*. The mood he's in, he'll take the place apart, and if he gets another assault charge he'll likely go to jail.'

'But if it was that important, why didn't he get me at the College, instead of bothering my friends?'

He stared at her. 'He's had a roadie outside the place, watching for you for weeks. And you weren't there.'

She looked in astonishment, and then, suddenly, it was clear. She got there earlier and left later than the other students. And then, they hadn't got a photograph of her. There were so many girls with long fair hair. And she very often tucked hers away in a woolly hat. She opened her mouth to explain, and shut it hastily.

She said, 'I don't want my friends pestered any more. It's not fair.' No wonder she had not heard anything from Carole for weeks.

'In that case you'd better tell us where you're living.'

She said, softly, furiously. 'Mr Hopkins, this may be difficult for you to believe, but I don't want anything to do with Paul Devlin. I never want to see him again.'

'What about me, Cathy?'

'Or you, Chris. I don't want to know you, Dev, or Easy Connection!'

She glanced round the table and saw that Lisa's friendliness had disappeared and Keith Hurst was looking at her, blackly hostile.

'Just as soon as this set ends I am going to walk out of here and forget this whole ghastly business. This has been the second worst evening of my life. It was sheer bad luck we met again.'

'You want to break him up completely?' Chris leaned forward, urgently.

She smiled without amusement. 'Don't be funny, Chris. I'm just a new toy for Dev. In another month he won't remember who I am. Look, Mr Hopkins, I'm only seventeen. I just want to be left alone to get on with my work. Please keep him away from me.'

He laughed grimly. 'Tell me how.'

'Couldn't you find him a girl? A model ... someone like Chris's girl?'

She saw Lisa, Keith and Bill Hopkins looking at her curiously, with an odd pitying expression, as though she hadn't understood anything at all. Then she met Chris's eyes, and was shocked at their blaze of fury.

'I make do, Cathy. You think it's what I want? What Dev wants?'

She was remembering what they had done to her. 'I'm sorry, I don't care what you and Dev want. To me you're not real people. You're just something the newspapers write about. I'm not a worshipper in your temple.'

She turned her shoulder on the angry outburst of argument, not listening, holding Nick's hand hard to stop herself bursting into tears. It was all right if you didn't actually start crying.

Night Mission had got back on the stand with Dev, amid cheers and whistles. They sorted themselves out and began to play an old Easy Connection classic, *Red Rock*.

By the time they were into their second piece, everybody realized that something extraordinary was happening. Night Mission, always an excellent band, had already been putting on a peak performance. And now Dev, a superb guitarist on record, an electrifying performer live, was giving an incredible display of virtuoso playing, stimulated by an explosive compound of vodka, fury, desire, joy and the knowledge that Cathy was there, watching him play for the first time.

After one startled glance at him, Dave Hampton flung himself into the music, pitting his own skill against Dev's, who, in turn, reacted by playing even more incredibly. And so it went on, building up, the audience getting more and more excited. They were all standing up now, the tables had been pushed back against the walls and everybody had crowded to the front.

The session became legendary overnight. Fortunately there was a recording enthusiast in the kitchen at Azra's. The L.P. issued later went to the top of the album charts, and became a classic.

For a while even Cathy forgot everything except the music. There was a roaring excitement in Night Mission, and there was Dev. She had not imagined that the brooding power which so frightened her would transform into this flashing, cat-like litheness. Had not imagined that his dark-gold beauty could become so electrically alive that she could not look away from him.

She slid her hand away from Nick, clutching her sketchbook to her, breathing shallowly.

*If only she could paint this!* All of it. The driving excitement, the atmosphere, and the musicians. Dave Hampton, craggy and dark, laughing aloud with the joy of playing to his fullest abilities, and Dev, with the line of his arching back, tilted head, and his arm outstretched, the long, powerful fingers apart, as he flung out the chord sequences.

She had said she was not a worshipper, but Dev's playing was penetrating her feelings more deeply than she wanted to understand.

An hour and a half had gone and the performance was nearly over. Dave Hampton announced their last number. The band was looking utterly exhausted. Their hair dripped, and both Dave and Dev had thrown off their soaking shirts and were naked to their hips, their bodies shining with perspiration.

'Nick,' said Cathy, speaking close to his ear. 'Please, we must go, as soon as they stop. I don't want to have to speak to Dev again.

Please?' She shivered, suddenly terrified, thinking about the state he would be in when he finished.

Nick saw her anxious face and squeezed her hand. 'Don't worry, Cathy. We'll go after the first encore. We'll move along the wall to the back. There's more room there and we'll be first out of the door. We kept our bargain, and wasn't it worth it!'

'I wish we could go now.'

'They'd all notice. You don't want another scene with his manager, do you?'

'It's Dev I'm frightened of.'

'Don't be silly, Cathy. After all, what can he do to you?'

She looked away quickly, but not before he had seen her eyes. For no reason at all a cold feeling moved down his spine.

Then the band were into their final number, *Gale Force*. It started slow, and low, with the various instruments talking to each other in solos, and built up over nine minutes, into a rushing, crashing, crescendo of sound, faster and faster, then dropped to nothing, then to the small curling sound of a clarinet.

The audience went crazy, shouting, yelling for more, an encore, stamping their feet, hammering on the walls and tables.

The band, haggard, grinning, suddenly conscious of their exhaustion, made a superhuman effort, and *Gale Force* swept again to its overpowering climax.

'Now!' said Nick, as the music ended and the applause started. Nick and Cathy edged along the short distance of wall to reach the back of the crowd.

What happened then was never fully clear. There was a vicious yell behind them – more closely resembling a scream – and as they spun round, Cathy met Dev's mad, furious eyes over the heads of the surging, screaming audience. He yelled something else, which she could not understand, and the next moment he had leapt towards them off the stand, ploughing through the people crammed near the stage. It was uncanny the way he had known they were leaving.

The fans, thinking he was either trying to escape without another encore, or that he had been hauled off the stand, closed their ranks and hung on to him, supporting him, laughing.

Dev, mad with fury, laid about him with his fists and made some headway before going down in a flurry of fighting, kicking bodies

Cathy, frozen, appalled, stood for a second, as the room exploded into violence. The extraordinary excitement generated throughout the evening finally blew up, and everywhere people were fighting, breaking up chairs and throwing over the heavy wooden tables. Then Nick caught her hand and they were away up the stairs and half-way down the street before two police cars passed them and skidded to a halt outside the Club.

# Eight

They walked home. Cathy felt Nick's distance. He did not speak or look at her.

At last she said quietly, 'I'm sorry.'

'You could have told me.'

'I can't ... talk about it. Something happens to my throat ...'

'Try.' His voice was hard. She realized how hurt and angry he was. She struggled to find a way to speak, to explain.

'I thought it was all over. I thought I could forget it all.'

'The sleeping – at the beginning – when you were so uptight, that was part of it?'

'Yes.'

'Part of *what*, Cathy?'

There was a long silence; twice she started to speak, and stopped. Under a street light he pulled her round to face him. *'I want to know.'*

She stared at him desperately, sick with the taste of blood.

'Have you made love with Chris *and* Dev, or only Dev?' His voice was cold, judging.

'I ... I haven't ... Dev ...' The words stuck in her throat. 'I've been with Dev.' Her voice was so low he could hardly hear it.

'And Chris?'

'No! He's not even kissed me!'

He walked on, and with a sickening lurch of her heart, she realized he did not believe her. The trust that had grown between them had been shattered by Dev. Like a car windscreen, she thought. Not repairable. She began to shake.

'How long?'

'You don't understand! It's not like you think. I only met them once, and then Dev for half an hour.'

He did not reply and she wondered if he had even been listening, when he said quietly. 'You belong to them. Both of them. Chris as well as Dev.'

'It's not true! You're crazy!' But the red dates in her diary suddenly spun into her mind. She pushed her shaking hands into her pockets.

'Cathy, don't you see, you're *already* one of them. Have you any idea what the three of you are like together? You . . . complete them.'

'Nick, oh Nick! Please don't say things like that. I know you're hurt, but honestly, you don't understand. I'm so frightened of Dev. If only I could explain . . .'

The bright hopes, the happiness of the last few months were falling apart and there was nothing she could do.

She began to cry, quietly, hopelessly. He put his arm round her gently and she leaned her head against his shoulder.

'I love you, Nick.'

There was a long silence and then he took his arm away from her.

'You don't, Cathy. You think you do. Yesterday I thought so too, before I saw you with them. But now . . . I'm nothing. I couldn't compete with those two. Dev said I was outclassed and he's right. They . . . they're fantastic.'

She heard, with shock, something in his voice which came close to hero worship. She remembered that he had collected every one of their records, that he had once wanted to be a rock star himself. She began shivering again, and could not stop. The iciness clamped down.

Nick said, 'It's not the money and way they look. It's their freedom, their music, their style. Most of us are just bystanders. *They are the ones we watch living their lives.* They're just what I always wanted to be, Cathy.'

She turned her head away, letting the tears run, but they could not ease the pain of rejection. He wanted Dev to have her. He didn't want her himself.

'I knew I couldn't win. I saw you watching Dev while he was playing.'

She drew a deep breath. 'You still don't understand, Nick. There wasn't any competition. You'd already won. But it doesn't matter now.'

She turned and walked away from him.

*

The next day the Sunday papers carried a photograph of Dev, Chris, Keith Hurst and Dave Hampton, pushing angrily through a crowd of youths, reporters and police.

*Night Mission – Easy Connection riot.*

There was little news, so it had big coverage. Fifty people arrested. Fifteen thousand pounds of damage.

'Fifteen thousand pounds!' Cathy was astonished. 'All those old chairs and tables? And the walls are emulsioned!' She was reading the paper over Nick's shoulder at the kitchen table.

He grinned. 'That's how much Azra's hoping to screw out of the insurance company.'

'But it's not fair. It makes it sound worse than it really was.'

Dev was charged with being drunk and disorderly and insulting behaviour at the police station.

Nick laughed. 'Drunk and disorderly. That's good! He had laid out two blokes before we left. That's assult. Bill Hopkins must be a *very* good manager.'

Inside the paper there was an editorial about violence, linking the riot with football hooligans and racial attacks.

'It's not fair,' she said again. 'They get the blame and they were only playing music.'

'Dev started the fight – you know he did.'

'It was my fault really, because I wanted to leave.'

He did not look at her. On the surface, things were back to normal this morning, but the old understanding had gone and there was a new formality which had never been there before.

'There's a bit in the gossip column you ought to see.' He turned back the page.

*Girl-about-Town writes: 'It was quite a night at Azra's, with the place jumping even before the riot. The Club, an exclusive West End nighterie, is the latest and trendiest hideaway for the jet-set. Tired celebrities jammed the club, to hear Night Mission, fresh from its U.S. triumphs. Among the audience was Easy Connection's Chris Carter, squiring Samantha Smithson-Black, only daughter of Lord Linton, the property developer.*

Cathy grinned, involuntarily, remembering Dev's rude introduction.

*'Keith Hurst – unstoned, surprise, surprise! – held hands with a very*

*pregnant brunette and Paul Devlin announced to all and sundry that he was about to enter the matrimonial stakes with stunning blonde girl friend, Katherine Marlow. Don't get excited fans. Who is Kathy? What is she? No one seems to know. Bill Hopkins, Connection's manager, told me, grinning, "He fancied the girl at the next table – who wouldn't? – and gave her a kiss or two. Dev was feeling very happy with himself and wanted to spread it around a bit!" You can spread some of it this way, any time you like Dev!'*

Cathy stared at the paragraph and read it through again, more slowly. She saw now what Chris meant about the way the media changed the way things really were. Everything had been subtly changed. The important things left out. Why didn't they say Keith was with his wife? They had implied too that he was always on drugs. It was amusing to hear poor old Azra's place called an exclusive nighterie, when they had only just stopped selling brown rice and vegetable quiche.

'It's not how it was at all. They haven't even spelt my name right – thank goodness. You're right, Nick. Mr Hopkins is really clever.' She glanced up, surprised. Nick had already gone.

# Nine

It was Sunday afternoon. The heavy Sunday quiet closed down like a fur muff.

Bernard had disappeared after lunch. Julie went off to a museum with a sketchbook and Alun was playing Bach in his room, looking at the ceiling and waiting for something to come through, so he said, when she asked if he wanted coffee.

And Nick was stretched out on the sofa in the living room, sleeping. Much too long for the sofa, he had managed to fold himself into its space by putting his head on its arm, his face turned away, his chest turned the other way, one arm trailing on the floor. One leg was stretched out over the sofa arm and the other leg was bent and turned inwards.

Cathy watched him lovingly for some time, noting the line of his chin and shoulder, the turn of the knee. He was utterly relaxed, no tension anywhere in his body. It was a beautiful pose, but so difficult to draw with its constant changes of direction. Then, unable to resist, she fetched her drawing block and pencil and began to struggle with the conflicting rhythms and directions of movement. It was even more difficult than the pose in the life class that week.

Bernard came back, put his head round the door, winked at Cathy and went away, his eyes abstracted. He's got an idea, thought Cathy, pleased. Bernard had been going through a difficult time lately. She drew on, looking hard, working carefully across the whole page.

It was a nuisance about Nick's shirt, though, she thought. She really couldn't see the muscle layer properly.

After half an hour Nick opened one eye and she realized that he had not been asleep all the time.

He said, without moving: 'Do you want me to take off my shirt?'

'Do you mind? I can't get the twist of the body at the diaphragm.'

He got up, unbuttoned his shirt, dropped it carelessly on the floor and got back on the sofa in the exact position.

'That's clever.'

He grinned. 'I've done some modelling for the College.'

She saw at once how hopelessly wrong her drawing was. The interplay of the ribs and muscles was much more complex and subtle. The pencil was no good now; she needed to work larger, using tone to catch the light falling on the skin.

She fetched her drawing board, some large sheets of cartridge paper and conté crayon.

'You look marvellous.' She balanced her board on the back of another chair. 'How did you get like that?'

He smiled. 'Working on a building site most of the summer. It's very good for the physique. Gives you a nice tan to pull the birds with, too.'

She looked down, pierced with jealousy. Other girls. Not her now.

She began to draw rapidly, furiously, concentrating entirely on getting the relaxed energy of the muscular forms on to the thick paper. The bone structure never bothered her now. The strong black lines bit into the paper, crossed and recrossed, an intricate network of conflicting movement.

'Are you tired? Do you want to move?'

'I'm all right.'

She started another drawing and this time the now familiar forms began to flow on to the paper, interlocking, simple, effortless. She drew a deep breath. *This* is what she had struggled for all these weeks, and now for the first time, it was happening. Like the Zen drawings. Simplicity, complexity, energy, relaxation.

She dropped the finished drawing and quickly altered her position to a new angle to add foreshortening to the problems, but it made no difference. The lines and forms came together effortlessly, *inevitably*. She could see so clearly what to do next. It was like flying. She wanted to laugh with exhilaration. Her arm was tensing with excitement, and she stopped for a moment to shake it into looseness again.

Outside, the afternoon was rapidly darkening, and she realized she could hardly see the paper.

'Well, well. What a very cosy, domestic scene!' Dev said, behind her. 'Life among the artists!'

She started so violently that the piece of conté crayon sprang out of her hand, exploding into pieces on the stone hearth. She put her board down carefully, and went over and collected up the broken pieces. Her knees and hands were shaking. She did not know why she felt so badly about Dev seeing her with Nick like this. She felt odd, almost guilty, as though she had been doing something wrong.

Dev had picked up her drawings and was studying them, comparing the drawings with the original.

'Mm. Very *good*. A splendid model. A splendid drawing.' His voice was savage. 'Lots of loving detail.'

She flushed brilliantly.

'Where are your drawings of *her*?'

'There aren't any,' said Nick, evenly. 'I'm interested in light refraction.' He pulled on his shirt. 'We haven't been making love, if that's what you're implying.'

'You hadn't got round to it yet?'

Cathy was suddenly, violently angry. How dare he try to put them in the wrong? *He* was the one who had done wrong, and now he was trying to destroy maybe her last chance of happiness with someone she really liked, and all for no reason other than greed and malice.

She looked hard at Nick. 'How did *he* get here?'

'I gave the address to Bill Hopkins.'

She breathed slowly, deeply, trying to control her anger. In a while, she thought, I shall be raving and screaming.

'*Why?*'

'Why not?'

'You knew I didn't want to see him again.'

'There's no reason for you to be hiding.'

'No reason?' She began to laugh, hysterically. '*No reason?* Are you mad? You think I want him walking into my room when he feels like it? You think I want more public scenes like last night? Don't you understand, Nick? He's capable of anything, anything at all.'

'Calm down, Cathy. You're getting hysterical. If you don't want to see him, you tell him and he'll go away.'

She stared at Nick for a long moment, dangerously, then she spun on her heel and flung open the living room door, hysterical laughter still shaking her voice.

'Thank you so much for coming, Mr Devlin. But your attentions are unwanted and unacceptable. I should be glad if you would go and not return. Not ever . . .'

To her fury, tears blinded her, and she dashed them away with the back of her hand. 'Please? Please? *Please*, Dev. Go away. Leave me alone. Let me get on with my life.'

Dev was half-sitting, half-leaning on the large table, smoking a cigarette, elegant in a pale grey suede suit and white silk shirt.

He looked at her for a moment. Then, with that rapid decisive movement that she remembered so well, he threw the cigarette into the fireplace and walked across the room to the door and snapped on the light. He looked tense.

'Where's your coat, Cathy?'

'Coat?'

'I'll take you home. You know we have to talk.'

'I am home and there's nothing we have to talk about.'

He went absolutely still, dangerous, like a cat about to spring. 'You mean this is your address, as well as his? You are living here with him?'

'That's right. I'm living here. Now, just go away and mind your own business. It's nothing to do with you.'

He laughed unpleasantly and sat down on the sofa. He stretched out his legs and put his hands behind his head, watching her.

'You'll have to forget him.'

'No.'

'I told you yesterday it was over.'

She turned away, and Nick saw her hands shaking.

'We've got to talk. You want him to hear?'

'There's nothing to talk about. There's nothing he can't hear.'

Nick went and closed the door. 'Don't you think you ought to tell me what's between you, Cathy?' he said, quietly. 'Why are you so frightened of him?'

'There's nothing between us.' Cathy's voice was bleak. 'It was all over months ago.'

He looked at Dev.

'Rape.' Dev smiled lazily, amused at Nick's expression. 'I raped her. Hasn't she told you?'

98

Nick glanced at Cathy's still iciness and back at Dev, his anger rising.

'Not much of a joke.'

'No joke.'

'Cathy! It's not true ...'

She leaned her head on the door, and he saw tears running down her cheeks. He knew now why she couldn't talk about it. He wanted to go over and put his arms round her.

'Cathy ...'

'There's something else,' said Dev, 'which she won't admit even to herself.'

Nick looked at her. 'What something else?'

'Nothing.' She had stopped crying. 'There's nothing.'

He looked back at Dev.

'Loving. Afterwards she loved me.'

'No!'

Dev ignored her. He was looking at Nick.

'You know she's having my baby? That she's two months pregnant?'

Nick looked stunned. 'Cathy! You didn't say ...'

'I'm not. I'm not. It's not true.'

Dev was suddenly on his feet. He caught her shoulders and pushed her chin up so that she was forced to look into his eyes.

'You're a liar. When was your last period?'

'That doesn't mean anything!' she said desperately, trying to pull away. 'I've been worried, upset. It could be that.'

'Twice?'

'It couldn't happen like that! It couldn't. Not the first time.'

'It can, and it has. Cathy, you've got my baby inside you.'

Her heart seemed to turn over. She closed her eyelids to shut out the hot darkness of his eyes. He bent his head and kissed her on her mouth. Cathy was trembling. Nick looked away.

'You've got to see a doctor, Cathy. I'll fix it for you,' Dev said.

She stood away from him, a fine perspiration beading her forehead. The colour drained from her skin.

'Get rid of it, you mean?' She laughed harshly. 'I hadn't thought. Of course, you would know about things like that. It must happen all the time to you. Bill Hopkins has probably got a special fund!'

99

Dev stared at her dangerously for a moment. He took a step forward and Nick thought he was going to hit her. Then he spun on his heel and walked away. He lit one of his long black and gold cigarettes with a shaking hand and threw the packet across the table to Nick.

'Sorry to disappoint you, Cathy. I didn't mean that. I'm not paying for an abortion. The need doesn't arise. I'm marrying you instead.'

She began to collect her things, angry, contemptuous.

'You've been drinking again. Or drugging. Go home and sleep it off!'

He smiled coolly. 'December 1st, in Nethercombe Parish Church. I've been on to your brother and the Vicar.'

She drew an unsteady breath, controlled herself and turned to the door. 'You are *raving*.'

He moved in front of her, his eyes like black fire.

'Listen, I want that baby. Do you hear me? It's mine. I asked the Atlantis stone for it. I've never asked the stone for anything I've really wanted without getting it. And you broke the cord. It'll be a boy. I want ... my ... son!'

She remembered Chris saying he was superstitious. It was incredible. He couldn't *really* believe the Atlantis stone could make wishes come true. *But how had he known she was pregnant?* For a moment she felt again the strange whirling darkness she had felt when she wished on the stone. She felt its cool oval shape between her fingers. There was a coldness at the base of her spine.

Then anger rose in her, bitter and icy.

'No,' her voice was like stone. 'If I'm pregnant it's for me to decide what to do about it. You don't come into it at all.'

'Try and keep me out. I'm his father.'

'Suppose I say you're not?'

He laughed. 'Don't try that one, Cathy. Who else is there? There hasn't been time. This guy? He knew nothing about it, and if he thought it was his he'd have tried to put me down before now. When the baby's born we can get a blood test. I've got a rare blood group.'

'Whatever its blood group, it will be nothing to you. Even I know that the mother has sole rights over an illegitimate child.'

'He won't be illegitimate. I told you, I'm marrying you.'

'You're mad. I'm seventeen. I'm not marrying anyone. I've got my work to do.'

'With a baby to look after? How are you going to earn a living? you won't be able to continue your course at the College even.'

'I – I'll put it with foster parents, get it adopted.' Her voice shook. She felt she was losing control. He was making her face the problems she had not been able to think about.

'If you do that,' he said grimly, 'I'll apply to the court for care and custody, and as you've no financial means of support I don't reckon they'll argue.'

'And what about your reputation? Your kind of life? You think drink and drugs and half-naked girls, and rock music, are good for bringing up babies?'

He laughed. 'Money is a great whitewasher. A farm in the country. Respectable housekeeper. A nurse and a nanny. A rich, loving father. Against a schoolgirl mother, studying *art*, with no job, no home, no money. Shacking up with another student . . .'

'We're not,' said Nick, suddenly, determined.

Dev turned slowly, as though he had forgotten Nick was there, and raised an eyebrow.

'Not living together. There are five of us sharing this flat, three men and two girls. We've got our own rooms – and we stay in them.'

Dev turned back to Cathy. His eyes gleamed mockingly.

'Trying to make me jealous?'

She was pale. Treachery again. She could take most things, but not disloyalty, not treachery. Nick was frightened, she thought. After today there would be nothing left for them.

'Trying to make you understand that I don't want anything to do with you.'

He was bored. 'For Chrissakes, Cathy, how long are you going to keep this up? You know perfectly well that marrying me will solve all the problems. You can have the baby with the best attention. He can be looked after by a nanny, and you can go on painting if you want to. Even continue the course after the kid's born. You can drive up to the old Col every day in the Bentley. Think of that!' He laughed.

She looked at him with hatred. Hating his calm assurance that he had only to make a decision, and everybody would get into line. Hating his lack of remorse. Hating him for breaking up her all too brief, gentle love. Hating him for his laughter and arrogance and assumption that everything could be bought with his money.

'You haven't listened to anything I've said so far. Dev, whatever happens to me will *never be anything to do with you*! I wouldn't marry you if you were the last man in London with the last tube of paint!'

A muscle moved in his jaw. 'Very dramatic.'

'The *truth*. You think I want to make everything worse, ruin my life completely, by marrying one of *Easy Connection*? Your life is like a surrealist horror film to me. How could I do my work properly, living like a goldfish? The newspapers, the publicity, the girls, the drugs ...'

'We've been straight for nearly two years,' he said angrily. 'Get used to the idea, Cathy, because it's going to happen anyway.'

'You think I can forget – just like that – what you did? Do you realize you can't even kiss me without me feeling sick?'

His eyes were unreadable. 'You'll get used to me.'

'I'll get an abortion!' she said wildly. 'It's the best solution.'

He caught her shoulders, his eyes glinting fury.

'Listen, Cathy. Listen good. If you get rid of this baby, I swear I'll give you another!'

She stared at him, ashen. 'Y-you w-wouldn't. Not even you would be so ...'

'Just don't get rid of it, that's all.'

He went out, slamming the door.

'Are you all right?'

'Yes.'

'I saw the light on. Can I get you anything, tea or milk or something?'

She was sitting on the side of her divan, fully dressed, with a blanket huddled round her shoulders. She looked dreadful, her face thin and white with huge black circles round her eyes.

'No, thanks.'

'You'd feel better if you had something.'

She swallowed hard. 'Don't be kind to me, Nick. I can't take kindness, just now.'

'Then come on out to the kitchen. It's warmer there. I'm opening a tin of soup.'

The soup was warm and comforting. She sat, holding the mug between her hands, looking so vulnerable that his heart twisted with pity.

'I'm sorry, Cathy, about everything.'

'Yes. I'm sorry too. About us. Since I started at College I've been happier than I've ever been before. I suppose I always knew it wouldn't last.'

'This is a bad patch. Things will work out.'

'People always say that when they're on the sidelines.'

He looked embarrassed. 'If there's anything I can do to help . . .'

'No. You don't want to get involved. I don't blame you.'

'It's not that exactly. You belong to Dev. He has a claim on you.'

'Nick, I truly didn't know about the baby. Don't know for sure now. I wasn't trying to fool you. You see, I just can't accept it. That's the most awful thing. When I try to consider what to do, a kind of barrier comes down, and all I can do is remember . . . the night it happened. And then I can't think at all. It's like a nightmare. The only real thing is my work.'

'What are you going to do, Cathy?'

'I don't know. All I can think is to go on with my work. I don't want to know about anything else.'

'Dev's right. You'll have to see a doctor, whatever you decide.' There was a long silence. 'Cathy, couldn't you go along with him? It's the easiest solution.'

She stood up. He saw she was shaking and cursed himself for a fool.

'It's no solution for me. I won't marry him. I hate him.'

'Are you sure? He said you loved him, that night – was that true?'

The colour came up brilliantly under her skin and she looked away. He thought she would not answer, but at last she said, 'Yes.'

'And when he kissed you today, you were trembling. Why?'

'I don't know!' she said, desperately. 'I don't know why he has that effect on me. That's why I'm ashamed and confused. How can it be like that when he did what he did?'

103

'He won't let you go,' said Nick. 'He's used to getting what he wants and he wants you badly.'

'He wants the baby. It's all mixed up with that stone he wears. He's superstitious.'

Nick looked at her. 'If you won't marry him, you know the only answer is abortion.'

'I can't face that idea yet. And Dev said ...'

'You don't really think he would.'

'He's very strong. I couldn't stop him.' She looked utterly exhausted.

'Come on, Cathy, you've got to get some sleep.'

'I won't wake up tomorrow morning.'

'Take tomorrow off. If you don't calm down, they'll be carting you off to the mental hospital – not the maternity ward.'

She smiled up at him, suddenly. 'Thanks for the soup – and thanks for everything else, too, Nick. You'll never know how much you've helped me. I wish ...'

At the door, she stopped, her back to him. Her voice was husky.

'Nick, the others ... they'll have to know about the baby, but ... please, you won't say anything, will you? I mean, about the ... way it happened? I couldn't bear anyone else to know. I feel so dirty and stupid.'

'Of course I won't say anything, Cathy. It's not my business.'

'No, it isn't. Thanks again, Nick.' She went out quickly before he could see the tears in her eyes; before he could see how much she still loved him.

# Ten

She woke late, to an empty flat. She had a bath, dressed, made breakfast, read an art magazine. Then, feeling better and calmer, she made telephone calls.

The first to the Vicar of St Michael's Church at Nethercombe, cancelling the wedding arrangements. This was more difficult than she anticipated, because the Vicar was very taken with the idea of a rock star marrying in his church, and even more with the publicity it would bring to his Restoration Fund. He was very curious. In the end she had to pretend to be Dev's secretary, and said that he would be writing to explain more fully.

The second call, to her brother, was even more difficult.

'Oh, thank goodness you phoned,' said Mary. 'We tried to get you all day yesterday, but the number was engaged all the time.'

'That's Alun,' said Cathy. 'He can't stand the phone ringing when he's working. He takes the receiver off.'

'He's no right,' said Mary, crossly. 'Suppose there's an emergency? It's been bad enough having to write to the College. Paul Devlin had to give us your number and address. I was so embarrassed! We've only heard from you twice since the term started. Why haven't you written?'

'I've been busy,' said Cathy, vaguely. 'Anyway, I didn't want Dev finding out where I was. You told him last time.'

'I'm sorry, Cathy. It all happened so quickly. I got flustered – with him standing there. I never *dreamed* . . .'

'Neither did I.'

'Cathy, is it true what Dev said?'

'I don't know what he said.'

'That you are having his baby, and you are marrying him in a few weeks' time in the Church here, and Jim is to be there to give you away. We couldn't believe it!'

'It may be true about the baby. But I'm not marrying Dev in St Michael's or anywhere else. That's what I wanted to tell Jim, but I suppose he's out as usual.'

'Checking a licence. But Cathy love, what are you going to do? Jim was so pleased about it . . .'

'*Pleased?* After what Dev did? Haven't you told Jim what happened?'

'Well, yes, I did. I had to. But he thought that everything could be explained . . .'

'You mean he thinks I *imagined* it?'

'No, of course not. I told him about your bruises, but he thinks it would be super for you to live in that marvellous house, with all the luxuries. We met Mrs Kaye, the housekeeper there, and she was telling us all about it. Jim thinks Dev must be a good person to stand by you, and be willing to marry you, although he's so famous.'

Cathy drew a long, deep, disbelieving breath, and gripped the receiver until her knuckles shone white.

'Just tell him I'm not marrying Dev, will you?'

'But what are you going to do?'

'I don't know,' said Cathy and rang off, before she lost her temper completely.

Then, taking another deep breath, she looked up the address of a pregnancy testing service in the telephone book, made another call, and in a few minutes, was walking towards the West End.

Afterwards she walked again. Down Tottenham Court Road, down Charing Cross Road, across Trafalgar Square, down Villiers Street to the Embankment and the Thames.

She walked along watching the silvery light on the water, smelling the odd, damp river smell, the barrier up in her mind, blanking off thought, except for the echo of the woman's voice.

'Positive. Positive, I'm afraid, dear. Are you all right? Do sit down, you look so pale.'

'Take the pamphlets,' the other woman had said. 'They'll tell you everything. The alternatives. You know you haven't got much time? It's a simple thing in the early days, but after sixteen weeks it's difficult, maybe an operation even, and scarring, and later on

it's illegal anyway. So do make up your mind *quickly* ... waiting
list ...'

'I'll let you know,' said Cathy.

Positive ... pos ... it ... ive ... pos ... it ... ive ... not ... much
... time ... not ... much ... time ... time ... much ... time. Her
heels banged the rhythm on the pavement stones, along the
Embankment to Westminster, past the Houses of Parliament, then
the river again.

She paused by Lambeth Bridge, imagining herself climbing on the
balustrade and jumping to the muddy water below. She wondered
how many girls like her had jumped into the river. It was a solution,
of a kind. If the police didn't fish you out first, it was a complete
solution.

Not for her, though, because she had work to do. Whatever
happened she must go on with her work. People would say that the
baby must come first, but this was not true for her. The work would
always be the most important thing in her life. She had not chosen
this – it was just the *truth*. She had never intended to have children,
knowing her work was her life.

She remembered the first time the knowledge had come to her.

She was sitting with her legs bent under her on a chair by the
window. It was New Year's Day. She was nine years old, and she
was wearing her new scarlet sweater. She was watching the first
snow falling.

She had been staring at the snow for a long time, aware of the
spaces between each snowflake, the distance between those close
to and those far away, feeling everything flowing downwards. It
had seemed for an odd moment that she was out there, hovering
among the snowflakes, but now they were flowing *upwards*.

There had been a television programme about the future, and
another part of her mind was thinking what she was going to be
when she was grown up, and why people were alive anyway.
Suddenly, with no warning, almost as though a voice had spoken,
the knowledge was there – that the whole reason and purpose of
her life was to paint pictures.

It was very strange, because, until that time, although she had
liked drawing and painting, and people at school had begun to keep
her drawings, it had not been especially important to her. She

hadn't even thought about being an artist. But there it was. The knowledge was clear, definite, indisputable. Later on, when she read about the way people had been 'called' to the church, she thought her own experience must be similar.

Since then, it had not always been as easy to accept. People did not understand. Her appearance was all wrong, they could not believe she was serious. Her mother had said, laughing, 'With your looks you'll get married and have a family.' And then later, 'You'll grow out of it.' And she had been forbidden to paint at home because of the mess. And later still her mother had said, angrily, 'You'll never make a living!'

Her friends grew bored and irritated. '*Why* have you got to stay and finish it *now*?' And boy friends drifted away when they realized they weren't really important to her. She had hoped that with Nick, who would surely understand . . .

Just last year, Jim had tried to make her leave school and get a job in an office, but the combined outrage and horror of the Head and her art teacher had defeated him.

It didn't matter what any of them said or did. She knew she would be an artist. She knew now that she had the ability to be a good one. Perhaps, even, if she worked hard enough, a great one.

Suddenly, she felt calmer than she had for several days, and she turned away from the river, aware for the first time of the cold November wind blowing against her face. Across the road, like a rock in the sea, was the Tate Gallery. Had she been walking towards this place instinctively?

She went across the road, smiling. Tomorrow, or maybe the day after, she would make a firm decision – adoption or abortion . . . or . . . or *something*. She would think it all out, but not now. Now she would look at paintings, think about her work and go back to College and draw out the largest canvas she had ever used. A new painting. The preliminary work was done, the studies were all pinned up, she had only to find the courage to start. Her heart lifted.

# *Eleven*

The next few weeks taught Cathy that no matter how bad the outward circumstances of her life, if her work was going well she could shut everything else away beyond that iron barrier of concentration and still be happy.

The set work on the theme of distortion was completed, and she was working on a series of paintings based on the distorting lenses she had found. These had been of single objects, then several objects, then the corner of a room seen through the lenses. Her latest painting was a metre and a half square. It showed her own room at Hamilton Square, but this painting was overlaid with objects of importance to her, seen individually in the lenses, blazing with a super-real colour and clarity, but as ghost-like as the room. The whole painting resembled a series of shifting veils of brilliant colour over a blurred image. It was complex, yet at the same time clear and serene. She wondered if she would ever be able to carry it through.

It represented to her the quality of the time and the life she had lived at the flat and her joy in her work. At the heart of the painting, reflected in a wavering glass bowl, she painted a tiny picture of Nick's hand, held out to help.

She had done over twenty-five studies in charcoal and colour for the painting, and a large number of lesser sketches and she worked with these spread around her and pinned on the division screen.

Her personal tutor, an austere, grey man, not given to praise, was impressed and said so. The Professor of Painting, himself a painter with an awe-inspiring international reputation, had walked past and looked at the painting for several minutes, and then had looked directly at her, intently, as though she was a *person*, not just a first-year student, beneath notice.

Tom Gibbon was one of the Visiting Artists – well-known professional artists who came round the College occasionally – not

teaching, but chatting cheerfully with the students. Althoug
he dressed in ragged teeshirts and jeans, and old training sho
with holes in the toes, he was currently one of the most fashio
able of the younger artists. His work sold for huge sums before
was even painted, and he had been a legend before he had le
College.

He too stopped at Cathy's easel and gave her that sharp co
sidering look. Then he sat down and looked at the painting properl
without saying anything, while Cathy fidgeted uncomfortabl
wishing he would speak.

'You got any more?'

'There's a few in the corner,' she said, uncertainly. 'There's som
on distortion and my life drawings. But they're only studies reall
This is the first of what I want to do.' Again, in silence he looke
through the paintings.

'Leaving this year?'

'No, I started in September.'

'First year! Great hopping fleas!'

She laughed and he regarded her kindly. 'You've done all thi
since September?'

'There's some more paintings at my lodgings, with life drawing
and, of course, there's the studies and work in the metal worksho
and the glass studio, and . . .'

'Stop! You're making me feel lazy.'

He stared at the painting again. 'Look, I know you won't wan
to sell now, because of the end-of-year assessments, but I'd like t
have that painting. So hang on to it for me, will you?'

She was scarlet with pleasure and embarrassment. 'If you'r
sure . . .'

'And I'll bring Caleb Crow along sometime. He'll be interested. H
likes to get to young talent before anyone else.'

She drew a breath. Caleb Crow of the Arundell Gallery, who pu
artists on contract, promoted them abroad, turned them into cele
brities, and who, by prodding, poking and irritating them, made
them produce work of a standard they did not believe they were
capable of.

She looked at him doubtfully. 'I'm not advanced enough. You'd
be wasting his time. I've got a long way to go.'

He laughed and got up. 'We all have. The best of us have even further to go. What's your name, love?'

'Catherine Harlow.'

'See you, Cathy!' He slouched away.

On Wednesday, a typewritten letter on thick cream paper arrived, saying that an appointment had been made for her on Thursday afternoon, at the request of Mr Paul Devlin. There was a Harley Street address die-stamped discreetly in the top corner. The doctor's name and qualifications took up two lines. Enclosed with the letter was a brochure advertising a book by the doctor, *The Joy of Motherhood*.

Cathy read them through expressionlessly and dropped them into the wastepaper basket.

There was an ominous silence surrounding Dev, explained by a postcard which arrived on Friday, postmarked Newcastle. The handwriting, unfamiliar, was black, large, spiky. It said, simply, 'December 1st, 2.30. St Michael's, Nethercombe. Be there.'

The card followed the letter into the waste bin.

She borrowed Nick's *Sounds* and looked up the list of tour dates. Sure enough, Easy Connection had been in Newcastle for a big concert on Thursday, and were in Manchester on Saturday, where twenty thousand tickets had been sold in two hours.

She breathed a sigh of relief. She was nervous of Dev's reaction when the cancelling of the wedding and the missed doctor's appointment got through to him, but for the moment it was certain that he was too involved to be thinking of anyone else.

Mary and Jim phoned, leaving messages for her to ring, but she ignored these and sank totally into her work, trying not to think of how little time was left to her.

# Twelve

On Saturday morning Cathy was roused by Julie banging on h
door and shouting for her to wake up because her brother was her

Jim looked unfamiliar in his best dark suit and white shirt. He wa
uncomfortable, glancing with distaste about the lounge and r
fusing to meet her eyes.

'I've got some business in town, Cathy, but I'll be finished by on
and I thought, well, Mary thought, you might like to come for th
weekend. I could pick you up and drive you down.'

'I can't spare the time.'

'We want to help. Mary is very worried. Cathy, you know we'v
got to talk things over. You need help. We want to do all we can.'

She looked at him, wearily. 'All right,' she said suddenly. She ha
to face them sooner or later, and it was true, she did need help.

Nethercombe again. She shivered. But Dev was in Manchester.

Mary was very pleased to see her. She began to cook a compli
cated meal from her glossy cookbook.

'I'm putting little Jimmy to bed while this is in the oven. Do yo
want to help bath him?'

'Bath Jimmy!' Cathy was incredulous.

Mary flushed. 'Well, I thought that now you might like ... i
doesn't matter!' She went out hastily.

Jim turned on the television, and they watched the inanities o
a quiz game and a panel game to the accompaniment of tempe
screams from the bathroom. It was clear that Jim had decided to le
her speak first, but when she showed no signs of doing so he go
more and more irritated. After a while Cathy got out the smal
sketchbook which fitted her shoulder bag and began to plan out he
next painting.

'How are you getting on at that College?' Jim's voice was hostile.

She told him about Tom Gibbon and his promise to bring Caleb ?ow to see her work, but he had never heard of Tom Gibbon or the ?rundell Gallery, and he could not understand how important it ?as.

'Anyway,' said Mary, coming back into the room, looking ex-?austed, 'you won't want to go on bothering about all that when ?e baby comes, will you?'

'Bothering! But Mary, it's my whole life!'

'You say that now,' Mary said complacently. 'You'll think dif-?rently when the baby comes.'

'Why?'

Mary looked astonished. 'Well, I mean, *art*. I suppose it's all right. ?ut what use is it?'

Cathy took a deep breath. 'It's important to me. I can't describe ? it's something I've just got to do ... like ... like eating or ?reathing. Don't put down my ideas, Mary. I don't put down yours.'

Jim said, angry, 'That's all very well, but what are you going to ?o about this baby? I'm your legal guardian and next of kin. I've ?ot a right to know.'

'I'm not sure yet. I can't ... adoption or ... or abortion. But I'm ?ot marrying Paul Devlin.'

'Why not, for God's sake?'

'*That* kind of man? Drink, drugs, girls. Marry the man who raped ?e?'

'I don't know that, do I? I only know what Mary told me.'

'Mary saw me.'

'She said you were bruised and hysterical. Girls are always hys-?erical about something or other. What's *your* story?'

'You *know*...' Cathy said, desperately, feeling her throat get tight. 'We had food and drinks and ... we talked. Then ... th-then ...' She ?oughed and swallowed. 'Dev took me outside and made me have ?ex.'

'Threatened to kill you? Beat you up? Spat on you? Kicked you? ?eed on you? Hit you round the head?'

'No! *No!* It wasn't anything like that!' She felt sick.

'That's rape, Cathy.'

'He did make me! He did!'

'Did you *say* you didn't want intercourse? You *told* him?'

113

'Of course I did ...' *Had* she? She felt she was losing control. can't remember. I was too upset, frightened.'

'You should have done. They always ask that in court.'

'But he must have known! I struggled ... tried to make hi stop ...'

'Why didn't you report it to me?'

'I knew you couldn't do anything. I wanted to get away – forg it happened!'

'Why didn't you see a doctor?'

'I didn't need to! *I didn't want anyone to know!*'

Mary said, sadly, 'Oh Cathy, I told you to. They can give you pill to bring your period on straight away. If only ...'

Jim said, disgusted, 'There's not a court in the country tha would convict him on that story. And nobody would believe either.'

'We're not in court! I'm just telling you why I'm not going t marry Dev!'

He looked at her and said, suddenly, 'How many times?'

Cathy stared at him, ashen.

'How many boys have you been with? Come on, let's have th truth. Girls who look like you aren't innocent virgins. You had boy friend at that comprehensive of yours. A kiss and cuddle afte the school disco, his hand up your skirt?'

Cathy's voice was hoarse, almost unrecognizable. 'I just don' believe this! I've not been with any boys. Steve and I, we never di anything. We just went to Ronnie's and S.W.P. meetings.'

'Honestly, Mary, if you'd seen her that afternoon. Her clothe sticking to her, her hair all over the place ...'

Cathy said wildly, 'You think I've been screwing around with everybody and got myself into this mess and I'm trying to pin it on Dev?'

There was a long silence and he stared at her narrowly.

'I'll tell you what I think. I think you drank too much and go drunk. That you went too far with him. That you got hysterical and panic-stricken and started to struggle and that he hurt you by accident.'

'*No!* That's not true!'

'You say it was the first time. The first time is always hard. Girls

114

never enjoy it. Even Mary . . .' He had gone brick red. 'Decent girls don't really enjoy it anyway.'

Astounded, Cathy looked at Mary. Mary had picked up the small garment she was making and began to knit quickly. She was very red.

Jim said ponderously, 'Over forty per cent of the rape cases we get are fake. In a lot of cases the girl provokes it.'

Cathy was nearly incoherent with rage. 'Fake or *never proved*? I know why men rape women. We read about it at school. It's because they hate and despise them. They think they're *nothing*. Dev just used me because I was a nothing.'

'He can't be so bad. He could just walk away and forget it happened. He doesn't have to marry you.'

'No. He could pay for an abortion and let me go free to get on with my work, but he wants the baby. It's all that money, isn't it? That's why you're defending him. It doesn't matter that I hate him. That I won't be able to work. That's not important.'

'You silly little bitch, you won't have to do another day's work in your life. Money cures a lot of ills.'

She looked at him. Heavy shoulders. Aggressive blue eyes. Her brother. Crude. Unfeeling. *Stupid*. How did they come to share the same parents?

She began to laugh, half-hysterically. 'It sounds like you need a good textbook about women, Jim. Mary might appreciate it too.'

'Shut up!' he said, viciously. 'She's not like you!'

White, Cathy got up and went to the door. 'Well, I think that says it all. I'm going to bed. No thanks, Mary, I don't want any food. I'll catch the early train tomorrow.'

'But you can't! We've . . .' Mary said urgently and stopped, as Jim looked at her. 'Oh well,' she ended lamely, 'we'll see.'

Cathy lay awake most of the night, racked with guilt and anxiety. Had it really happened the way she thought? Perhaps it *had* been her fault. Jim's hectoring voice echoed in her ears. But she had tried to stop Dev. She *had*.

Tired out, she slept long into the quiet of Sunday, waking too late to catch the bus and train she had intended. She was angry with Mary for letting her oversleep. The next bus which connected with the train was at two o'clock, and she was determined to be on it.

Jim glowered at her across the table as she ate her late lunch.

'You're acting like a ten-year-old. What have you decided?'

'I don't know! *I don't know!*' She pushed away her plate. 'Look Jim, *please* try to understand. Only a little while ago I was still a school, looking forward to college, and then suddenly, I'm having a baby, and everybody is talking about marriage. It's like a nightmare. I can't believe it. I'm not ready.' She put her head in her hands

Mary got up and put her arm round Cathy. 'Cathy, love, we all have to grow up sometime. Face up to our actions.'

'It's not fair. It wasn't my fault.'

'No, of course not. But you've got to decide what to do now. think you should reconsider marrying Dev. Cathy, he's the father of the child. And he can give you so much. That marvellous house Clothes, travel, servants, even. It's like a storybook ...' Mary flushed, seeing her expression. 'I don't think he's as bad as you imagine. He's very, very sorry about everything.'

'He's been here, hasn't he?' Cathy said softly, suddenly.

Mary glanced at Jim, uncomfortably. 'Well, yes, now you mention it, he has been here a couple of times. He explained to us how it happened, how he feels. You see he was very wound-up ... he hadn't been able to sleep, and he'd been drinking all day – well you know that. He says he really wanted you a lot. And he says you danced with him, and let him kiss you and seemed to be liking it ... and he kind of lost control ...'

'*My* fault!' Cathy said ironically.

'No! I know it was awful, but he really wants to make it up to you. I think you'd be happy.'

Cathy looked at her bitterly. 'So you've gone over to his side, too, Mary. It's the idea of abortion, isn't it? You're dead against that, aren't you?'

'Yes,' said Mary, quietly. 'You know I'm a Catholic, but if you had been a nurse and seen what I've seen you might be opposed to it too. The baby has a right to life.'

'It's not even born yet. It's not alive!' Cathy said wildly. 'You'd rather I had it hung round my neck like an albatross for the rest of my life?'

Mary said, defensively, tears in her eyes, 'Babies are babies and lovely, however they come.'

'Suppose,' said Cathy slowly, 'suppose I have the baby. Will you look after it while I finish my course and get a job? I'll get some money for its support and I'll pay it all over to you and come down at the weekends. You have little Jimmy, and you say you want to help. Won't you look after it for a while?'

Mary hesitated, looking at Jim.

'No!' he said, sharply. 'Why should we take over your responsibilities? The baby needs a father and you need a husband. Someone to take care of you both. Or it'll happen all over again with some penniless student who'll leave you flat. And what kind of job do you think you'll get when you finish that course?'

'If Caleb Crow likes my work . . .'

Jim snorted. 'We'll be supporting you both for years!'

Cathy said, white with fury, 'You've never given me money or support, Jim Harlow, and don't pretend you have. You're a hypocrite! All that stuff about wanting to help! I was a fool to think you meant it. All you wanted was to talk me into marrying Dev, so the scandal is hushed up and your boss doesn't get to hear of it! Somebody to take care of me? *I can take care of myself!*'

'Looks like it, doesn't it?'

She stared at him, and heard herself saying bitterly, unforgivably, 'It's all your fault. You knew I wanted to leave, that evening at Cox's Farm, but you were so frightened they would complain. You made me stay. You handed me over to them. *It's all your fault I'm in this mess!*'

She ignored the outburst of argument and stared out of the window. She saw, without surprise, Dev's big red car drawing up to the gate. Dev got out and came along the path. He looked tired but vividly alive. He must have been driving for hours down from Manchester.

She turned and stared at them. Mary flushed and looked away. Even Jim had the grace to look uncomfortable.

'You told him I would be here today?' She said quietly. 'I suppose he asked you to speak to me?'

'We want you to be happy. He's a nice bloke.'

'Did he tell you I feel sick when he touches me? That I love someone else?'

'No, I didn't, Cathy. It's not relevant.' Dev had come straight in through the back door, without knocking, like a member of th family. 'Mary, Jim.' His eyes went quickly from one to the other. Jim shook his head angrily.

Dev shrugged and spread out his long fingers ruefully.

Cathy turned away, picking up her coat and bag. 'I'm going.'

'I'm driving you back to town.'

'No, thanks. I'd rather catch the train.'

'You've missed the bus.'

She looked at the clock and saw he was right. So Jim had even planned that, in case Dev hadn't made it in time.

She looked bitterly at Jim. 'You sold me out. You're my brother, but you sold me out, *twice*. And you tried to stop me painting too. Don't write to me or ring me. I never want to speak to you again as long as you live.'

At the door she stopped, her back to the room. 'I thought you were my friend, Mary, but I was wrong about that too. I don't want to hear from you either.'

She went out and got into the car.

In a few minutes Dev followed, angrily slamming the door.

'They're very upset. You know something? I don't think I like you very much at the moment, Cathy.'

She smiled, whitely. 'Great. We're making progress.'

He started the car with a jerk, and then braked again.

'Put on the seat belt.'

She did not move, and he pulled the belt around her and clipped it in.

'Why blame *them*? It was my fault. I asked them to help.'

'They didn't have to agree. Your house, your fame, your money – *especially* your money, and they're eating out of your hand. Steve used to say that the police always licked rich men's boots. Well, Jim's a bootlicker all right. He'll be there, pulling his forelock as you drive up to the Big House ...'

'Shut up.'

'Look, Dev, *please* ... You've got to leave me alone. You're messing up everything. My career, my family ...' Her voice broke. 'Even Carole's mother wouldn't let me speak to her since your detective went round and bullied her.'

Dev glanced at her, annoyed. 'That wasn't your fault.'

'They're frightened I might involve Carole in bad company and drug-taking. You've no idea what Easy Connection means to ordinary people. You're like lepers or mad dogs with rabies to them.'

He flinched. 'Cathy, what makes you think I'm so tough I can take the terrible things you hand out so frequently?' He glanced at her and read her mind. 'Cathy, I'm not just a picture in the newspaper. I'm real. I'm a human being, and that *hurt*.'

She was ashamed, but her own pain was too raw.

'You must have been taking insults for years.'

'People don't normally say them to my face!'

Her bitterness and anger burned like a physical pain in her chest. She was furious with Dev for going behind her back and getting at her relatives, but it was Jim she felt most bitter about. The stupid, pompous, money-grabbing pig. She would never go back.

# Thirteen

Dev drove the powerful car skilfully, fast, but taking no chances. She huddled away from him, listening to the low purr of the engine, feeling the deep springing, the leather upholstery. It was a beautiful car. Like a TV ad. A girl, a car, and a beautiful young man to go with it. Sale of the Century, she thought. Yours for only two worthless pieces of paper: a marriage certificate and a birth certificate.

She stared out of the window at the early-darkening countryside, white still from the heavy frost of the night before. Each leaf seemed etched in silver, glittering in the low sun. It was a wonderland of silver, rose pink, and smokey shadows. As she looked, the pain drained slowly from her chest. No family now. No security. But there was this beauty. And there was painting.

She began thinking about her new painting.

'Cathy!' His voice was exasperated, and she realized he must have spoken several times before.

'I'm sorry?'

'Why didn't you keep the appointment in Harley Street?'

The attack had come unexpectedly, before she was ready.

'I ... how did you know I hadn't?' She was scared. 'You were in Newcastle, then Manchester, all tied up with concerts, so how could you ...?'

'They have phones up there, too, you know. If you think because I was doing a few gigs I wouldn't be thinking about the baby, you're way out. It's there at the back of my mind all the time.'

He drove on, and after a while, relieved, she heard him laughing. 'I was so angry with you in Manchester, I broke my favourite guitar. The audience thought I was doing a Pete Townsend, and went crackers.' He laughed again. 'You ought to come and see us sometime. Our stage act is pretty good. Lasers, dry ice, lights, flames, and Chris is fantastic.'

'You have a pretty good lead guitarist too.'

The car swerved slightly. 'Don't say you're handing out compliments now.'

'You don't need compliments. You know how good you are.'

'It's nice when other people think so too. Especially some people. You liked our jamming, the other night?'

'I thought it was brilliant. I never heard anything as good in any jazz club.'

'That was exceptional,' he admitted. 'Dave is really good.'

'You were better.'

He looked so delighted, so young and vulnerable, that she turned away, flushing. She had merely spoken the truth, without thinking, not intending to please.

She said abruptly. 'I'm sorry . . . I said . . . what I did, earlier.'

'Long knives and sweet honey,' he said softly. 'That's life with you, Cathy. But it's never boring.'

He looked at her sideways. 'Well, well, so you knew I was in Manchester. Perhaps we *are* making progress. How did you know that?'

'I looked it up in the paper. That's why I thought it would be all right to come down to Nethercombe.'

'Don't spoil it!'

After a while he said, casually, 'There's another appointment at Harley Street on Wednesday at three o'clock.'

'I'm not going.'

'I'll go with you.'

'I'm not going. I can't spare the time.'

The car slowed. He stared at her astonished and gave a shout of laughter.

'Cathy you are incredible. What are you doing that's so much more important than having a baby?'

'My work! There's so little time left. I've got to *work*. All right, go ahead and laugh. You all think it's a nice little hobby. But it's not like that for me. It's my whole life. It's the only thing I care about. You ought to know what I mean. You're the same about music aren't you?'

He did not answer. '*Aren't* you?' she persisted.

'Maybe. I thought so once. But there are a few other things too.'

'Not for me.'

'I know you are a good painter. I didn't know you were really dedicated.'

'Why should you?' She was surprised. 'You don't know anything about me. We don't know each other at all.'

'I know a lot. I know that you're clever, honest, serious, that you've got a sense of humour, that you're beautiful and sexy . . .'

'I'm not sexy!'

'I'm a better judge than you are, sweetheart!' he said, laughing.

Then he spun the wheel and drove into the forecourt of a road café.

'Why are we stopping?'

'I'm so tired, if I don't get a coffee soon, I'll drive off the road. Come on, I haven't had a proper meal since Wednesday.'

She remembered then that Chris had said he couldn't eat or sleep before a concert. She looked at him covertly as they crossed the forecourt. Although his eyes looked tired, there was none of that desperation she had seen at Cox's Farm or Azra's. He looked like the morning he had found her in her digs, twice as alive as most people.

It was a lorry drivers' café, nearly deserted at that time of day. Except for a man reading a newspaper in the far corner they had the place to themselves. Everything was brightly coloured, clean and plastic, brilliantly lit with neon strips.

'I wouldn't have thought this was your sort of place,' she said.

'Why not?'

'Not . . . exotic . . . enough.'

He laughed. 'When you know me better you'll find out that there's nothing exotic about me.'

He was wearing black velvet trousers, a high-necked shirt made of brilliant coloured satin patchwork, and a leather jacket trimmed with some strange long-haired fur. His long, dark-gold hair curled on his shoulders. She half-smiled. 'I'm a better judge than you are . . .' and stopped dead.

'Go on, you haven't finished it.'

To her horror, she felt herself blushing. He laughed again, and took his coat off, draping it over the chair back.

'Is that *monkey* fur?'

He grinned. 'I hope not, but I bought it in Africa.'

The elderly waitress waddled round the counter smiling.

'Nice to see you again, dear.'

'Hi, Emmy.'

'Where's the other boy?'

'Sleeping in.'

'I bet. You too?' She winked at Cathy, who went rosy red.

'Now then Emmy, none of that. This is Cathy, my intended. We're getting married soon.'

'Well!' She favoured Cathy with a comprehensive but sympathetic look. 'I'm glad to hear it. But I ain't read nothing about it in the papers.'

'It's a secret.'

'Well, the best of luck to you both. I reckon you'll need it more than most.'

She shuffled off with the order. Cathy, still red, looked at Dev.

'She knew about me. I didn't think it showed yet.'

'Just a bit. It's your skin and your hair. There's a special sort of glow.'

She looked down so that he shouldn't see the tears in her eyes. She was suddenly wildly upset. She was remembering Mary's glowing happiness when she had her baby. If only things had been different.

He stretched out his hands across the table and caught hers. He looked at her intently.

'Cathy, you're sure now, aren't you?'

She couldn't think properly. Electricity was pulsing through her hands and tingling up her arms.

'Y-yes. I took a test. It was positive.'

'When?'

'Monday.'

'You've known for a whole week without telling me? You're not being fair, Cathy. You know I've been worried. You could have phoned me. You let me go to Newcastle without knowing.'

She looked at him indignantly. 'I didn't know you were worried. Why should you be? I didn't know you were going up north, and I wouldn't know how to phone you anyway. I don't suppose you're in the phone book.'

He pulled her bag, lying on the table, to him, flicked it open, and shook the contents on to the table. With one long finger he hooked her diary from the debris of make-up, pens, pencils, charcoal, sable brushes and squashy rubbers. He flicked through the pages to the address section and wrote on a new page in his large, bold script, taking up the whole page.

'You've got a cheek!' she said, letting out her breath.

'That's my flat and phone in town. You know, girls *pay* to get hold of that? This is Cox's Farm and this is Bill Hopkins' office. If you ring they'll tell you where I am when I'm gigging.'

He sorted idly through the rest of the stuff from her handbag and pushed it all back, smiling.

'You are a pro, aren't you? More drawing stuff than make-up.'

'A handbag is private, like pockets.'

'Who are Brian Turner and Steve Banks? In your diary.'

She flushed scarlet. 'Mind your own business.'

'No secrets between husband and wife, Cathy.'

'They're boys I used to go out with. And I'm not your wife.'

'Soon.'

'No.'

'I'm jealous,' he said. 'I was never jealous of anyone in my life before. It's a new experience.'

She was angry, then amused at the absurdity.

'You going to show *your* address book to your wife?'

'If you want to see it, Cathy.'

'I said, your *wife*, Dev. I should think it's like an encyclopaedia – you know – twenty-four volumes.'

He pulled a small leather book out of his back pocket and pushed it over to her. 'Have a look.'

Red-faced she pushed it back. 'It's nothing to do with me.' Relieved, she saw that Emmy was bringing the food.

Cathy watched Dev eat an enormous plateful of eggs, sausages, baked beans, bacon and fried bread.

She laughed. 'I thought you had a delicate digestion. Didn't know you ate in places like this.'

'We practically lived in places like this when we first started,' said Dev. 'We were so broke we had to sleep in the van.'

'I'm not hungry,' said Cathy, 'I can't eat any more of this.'

'Give it here. I'll eat it.'

'I'll put it on your plate.'

He smiled at her. 'You got foot and mouth disease?'

He slid his empty plate away and pulled hers towards him. It was a small thing, but she felt very strange, watching him. It was the sort of thing families did, not strangers. But Dev wasn't a stranger. He was the father of her child.

She shivered and looked away. He made gestures to Emmy, who brought over another two mugs of coffee and a slab of raspberry tart and custard.

'You're surely not going to eat all that as well.'

He grinned. 'I haven't felt so hungry in years. Have some ice cream.'

She shook her head.

'It's all the exercise he's getting.' Emmy winked at Cathy. 'Got to keep his strength up.'

She went away laughing, and Cathy, to avoid looking at him, stared out of the window, her cheeks hot. He ate his tart slowly, watching her.

She tried to think of something to say, to break the speaking silences which had started to build up between them. We only need Chris, she thought, and it'd be like old times.

'D-did the concert go well in Newcastle?'

She thought. I sound like a woman's magazine on how to get your man – 'Show an interest in his hobbies' – or a wife, after a hard day . . .

'Not bad. But the fireworks are a menace at this time of the year. Some lunatics were throwing them about until Chris told them to cool it, and the fuzz carted off some guys. You always worry about people getting hurt.' He smiled gently. 'Why are you talking, Cathy? You know we don't need words.'

Her skin burned. 'I like to see you blushing. It really turns me on.'

She ignored him. 'I saw a good review of your new album in *Sounds*. They thought it was stupendous.'

'It's the best we've ever done. It'll go in at the top of the chart. We're pleased with it ourselves. You see, Cathy, we had two rocky years, really bad, when we thought we had hit bottom. Everybody said we were finished. There was Keith with his habit, a couple of nasty court cases, constant trouble with the police and press, and

I was . . .' He stopped dead. Cathy wondered if he would talk about the rich woman who had turned him into a neurotic wreck. He was looking blindly at the table. was he still in love with her? It seemed very likely. But after a few seconds he only said, 'Well, I had a lot of problems, too.'

'I couldn't come up with anything musically. But this year has been really great for us. We couldn't go wrong. The U.S. tour, the Scandinavian tour. I started to get good ideas again. Keith got off smack, found Lisa and married her and there's a baby due soon. And now I've got . . .' He stopped again, smiling at her.

She looked away. He wasn't going to blackmail her. She said, lightly. 'And now you've got a splendid new album all set to sell a million.'

'You know that's not what I was going to say, but it'll do for now.' He pushed his plate away. 'That was really nice.'

He stretched out his long legs, leaned back and put his hands behind his head, watching her. He looked extraordinarily attractive. The wild look was gone, and he seemed to be alive with energy and laughter, his eyes gleaming with flecks of golden light.

'You know, these places have a serious disadvantage. Now if this had been a hotel, we could have hired a room . . .'

She knew he was only saying it to embarrass her, but she could not prevent the colour flooding brilliantly into her face. She heard him laugh.

'If you have finished, perhaps we might go.' She stood up, refusing to look directly at him and went to the cloakroom, where she saw, looking critically in the mirror, that he had been right. You could see the baby. Her skin and hair. Her eyes were shining darkly violet. Her hair was like stiff gold. She combed it and tried to calm herself before walking back to the waiting car. It was like being possessed she thought. The baby was already taking over and changing her without her knowledge.

When they got back in the car their relationship seemed changed in some subtle way she could not understand.

He drove without speaking now and without looking at her. She stared out of the window and tried to think about her work, but there was a queer depth and dimension to the silence, and she could not concentrate. The silence seemed to grow and grow. She glanced sideways, saw his long-fingered hands moving casually over the wheel, and suddenly became paralysingly aware of him as a man.

Aware of the width of his shoulders, the bulk of his body, his slender hips, powerful thighs. She looked up and saw that he was watching her in the driving mirror. Their eyes linked, and her breath went away. A car passed them, too close, and at last she could look away.

She struggled to understand what had changed between them, but when the answer came she was so shaken she tried not to believe it. They had started the drive as two separate, hostile, people, but somehow, during the drive and the meal, the hostility had gone. Now there was an odd kind of companionship, wary but intimate. *They were finishing the drive as a couple.*

I won't let it happen, she thought, wildly. But it had happened already, constructed from all the small actions and sentences. Did he know? Of course he did! He had understood right from the beginning and had done everything he could to make it happen – eating from her plate, opening her handbag, telling the waitress they were getting married, everything to show they were a couple.

She glanced at him quickly, and once again their eyes linked. She tried to remember her hatred and fear, but it all slid away in his disturbing physical presence. She knew he was reading her as clearly as though she had spoken. She could feel his eyes drawing hers, demanding hers, but she would not look at him again, and tried to block her mind against him.

They drove through the outer suburbs, deeper into the heart of the grey city. On Westminster Bridge there was a tangle of traffic at the lights, and he leaned over and turned her face so that she must look at him. His eyes, very dark, moved over her, came back to her mouth, then her eyes. Her heart banged in her throat and all her skin seemed to be flowing with electricity from his hands. He looked at her searchingly for a long moment, his fingers moving gently against her neck.

Then, ahead, the traffic began to move and he turned to put the car into motion.

She thought, panicking, what am I going to do when we get to the flat? Suppose he insists on coming in? What am I going to do?

I can't handle him at all. She hid her giveaway hands under her arms and waited, frightened, while they turned into the old tree-shaded square and stopped outside number fifty-eight.

She said, politely, through dry lips, 'Th-thank you very much for bringing me home.'

He sat for a moment, staring ahead through the windscreen. Then he turned and looked at her again. She could not meet that dark, gleaming look at all now, knowing what he would read in her eyes, as well as in the silence. The trembling had started again, and her heart was thumping so hard she thought he must hear it.

'It's all right, I'm not coming in. I need some sleep.' She heard the smile in his voice. She fumbled for the car door, wondering if her legs would hold her upright on the pavement. He leaned across her and released the catch, enjoying her physical confusion. She leaned back as far as possible, but his mouth was an inch from hers. She closed her eyes, sure he would kiss her, quivering all over at the nearness of him.

He laughed, mockingly. 'Does Nick have this effect on you?'

She slid through the door and stood on the pavement.

'He hasn't practised on so many girls,' she said, and walked rather unsteadily across the pavement.

'Who's jealous now?' He called after her. He was still laughing as he slammed the door and drove away fast.

# *Fourteen*

Cathy was upset and confused. She distrusted and feared Dev, but she had never before felt anything like the intense physical effect he had on her. She had never imagined that her knees could turn to water and her whole being to jelly, just being near someone. It was nothing to do with *love*, but just remembering his fingers stroking her neck, she trembled all over again. It was true that Nick had never made her feel like that, and yet she knew she loved him. With Nick she felt secure and comfortable. With Dev she was as wary as a wild cat.

By the next morning, with Dev safely two miles and fourteen hours away, she was able to rationalize it very satisfactorily. After all, she had never met anyone even remotely as physically attractive as Dev, and in any case, there was nothing unique in what she felt for him. He had the same effect on thousands of girls all over the world. It really only showed how normal she was.

She was so pleased at this conclusion she went happily to the College, even earlier than usual, and by the time the lectures and classes started, she had sorted out the drawings and studies she needed for her new painting, and prepared the new, even larger, canvas.

She hammered in a corner piece more firmly and glanced from the canvas to the pinned-up studies. She needed the extra space, but she wondered if she was being too ambitious. She took a paint rag, a little green paint and some turps and began to rub it into the mocking white surface. It was to be a painting of that strange time, with Nick stretched out on the sofa, against the plants and the pin wall of the lounge. In her mind she already had a title for it. It was to be called *Sunday Afternoon*.

She attended two lectures, worked in the weaving department, had a long argument with Bernard and two other boys in the

College canteen about the morality of making art objects for rich men and museums, and late in the afternoon she returned to the studio to her new painting.

She put a few final touches to the painting of her room, which she called *September Song*, and started to draw out the design for *Sunday Afternoon*. The clear patterning of the shapes on the wall, the plants and objects, the central relaxed figure, began to flow together like her meditation drawings. She became increasingly excited as the design appeared on the canvas.

At last, she was too tired to go on. It was only eight-thirty, and normally she worked for another half-hour at least. But she realized that the baby was beginning to take her strength, and soon she would have to sit down more often, or even lie down in the afternoons. She pulled herself up sharply. *If she kept it, that is.*

She walked home slowly, elated, and full of a deep satisfaction. She grinned at her reflection in a shop window, which showed her hair falling down from being pinned up, a smudge of paint on her nose and another long streak of paint down the side of her cheek and chin. Her working jeans and shirt were full of paint too. It was a pity Dev couldn't see her now. It would put him off completely!

When she got in, Dev was playing chess with Alun in the lounge.

Not stopping she went straight on through to the kitchen where Julie was making coffee. She took a cup, filled it with cold water and drank it down.

'How long has *he* been here?'

Julie turned to her, her eyes excited. 'About an hour. Oh, Cathy, why didn't you say you were engaged to Paul Devlin of Easy Connection? You know they're my very favourite band and ...'

'I'm not,' said Cathy, wearily, leaning against the sink, all her lovely satisfaction melting away. 'Pregnant, but not engaged.'

Julie looked staggered. 'Pregnant! But *Cathy* ...'

'I know. I don't want to talk about it.'

'But Dev said ...'

'I don't care what he said. I wish you hadn't let him in.'

'Take no notice, Julie,' said Dev. He was leaning on the door frame. 'We're getting married at Nethercombe Church in a couple of weeks. It's all fixed.'

Cathy turned away and started to open a tin of soup. Even at a range of ten feet, the effect had begun to operate. She had to concentrate hard to prevent her hands from trembling.

'What do you want here?'

He came in and sat on the table, watching her. 'I came to take you out for a meal. Not a pull-up.'

'Thank you,' Cathy said, politely, as though to a total stranger. 'But I just got in. I'm too tired.'

Julie, who had been staring from one to the other, fascinated, was suddenly jolted into action.

'I'll take Alun's coffee,' she said. 'Your coffee is there, Dev.' She disappeared hastily, shutting the door.

Dev came over and stood behind Cathy as she waited for the soup on the cooker.

'Cathy.'

'Are you trying to destroy this place for me as well?'

'Cathy, look at me.'

'I don't want to.'

He kissed her bent neck, then along her chin, turned her to him, and slid his mouth on to hers. With an effort, she did not respond.

'You smell delicious. Turpentine and linseed oil.' He turned her face up, and saw her ringed eyes, the tiredness like a grey veil. 'Poor little baby. You're working too hard.'

'I have to. Time's running out.'

He kissed her again, lightly, gently. 'Go to bed. I'm not staying. I just wanted to see you.' He went away, leaving her shaky and wanting to cry.

'I'm sorry about last night,' she said to Julie, next day, seeing her in the canteen. 'I didn't mean to be grouchy. I was tired and I never expected to see him.'

Julie grinned. 'Poor Dev! If he was expecting a welcome he didn't get it. How can you treat him so offhand when he's so gorgeous? And he's crazy about you.'

Cathy shook her head. 'No. Most of it's a put-on. He wants the baby, you see, and he's afraid I'll decide not to have it, or have it and get it adopted. He'll even marry me for it.'

Julie shook her head. 'I don't think it's a put-on.'

'Oh, I think he quite likes me at the moment because I'm not

131

available. But he'd be bored with me in a month. Can you imagine what it would be like married to someone living Dev's kind of life? Crazy gigs, wild parties, tours for months, everybody watching you wherever you went, everything you do in the newspapers. And drink, drugs maybe, and all those girls? I just couldn't stand it. I must have a quiet life to get on with my work. I went to his place once, and there was this girl, Charis.' She told Julie about Charis. 'Can you imagine coming home and finding girls like that all over your house?'

'Oh, he wouldn't, Cathy!' Julie was shocked. 'Some of the rock stars have been married a long time.'

'Perhaps their wives don't care, with all that lovely money around. Can you imagine Dev and Chris living like monks on a three-month tour? I couldn't keep a man like Dev. When I get married I want it to last. I'd be waiting for Dev to divorce me all the time.'

Julie looked at her. 'You still fancy Nick, don't you?'

Cathy coloured and looked away. 'He doesn't want me, Julie. And then there's the baby.'

'What are you going to do?'

'People keep asking. I don't know yet.' The tension was back in her voice, and a note of near hysteria, which Julie failed to register. 'I'll think about it soon.'

Dev was at the flat again that night, playing cards with Nick and Bernard, and another boy from the College.

On Wednesday she went to the flat of a girl she was friendly with at College, and deliberately stayed very late, but when she got back he was still there.

She looked down at the lit, uncurtained room, and thought how happy and friendly everyone looked, as though there were no problems. Perhaps it was just *her*.

They were watching football on the television, waving and urging on the players. Bernard and Alun were on the floor. Several friends were sitting on the various chairs and Nick was on the sofa next to Julie. Next to Julie, on the arm of the sofa, with his arm lightly round her shoulders, was Chris Carter. Dev was in the big armchair facing the window, stretched out, pouring a can of beer into a glass. Then he raised his eyes and looked directly at her through the window. He put his glass on the floor and came out to meet her.

'You're late. Where have you been?'

She raised her eyebrows, annoyed, and hung her jacket on the peg.

'I was beginning to think you'd run away again.' He pulled her urgently against him and kissed her hard on the mouth. She pushed him away.

'Now then,' said Alun, coming out of the room, 'this 'ere's a respectable lodging, and we don't want none of your nasty showbiz 'abits corrupting our young ladies!'

He sounded so much like Diana, her old landlady, that Cathy was forced to smile.

Dev put his arm firmly around her waist, so that she had no chance of slipping away to her room. 'Come and have a beer, Cathy.'

'I'm just off to get some more booze. We'll make a night of it,' said Alun.

'Take my car.' Dev found his car keys in his back pocket and threw them to Alun. 'It'll be quicker.'

'Wow! You'll trust me with that pretty thing?'

'If you crash it, I'll kill you,' said Dev amiably, and pushed Cathy, resisting, into the room.

To her surprise, Chris came over and kissed her lightly on the forehead. 'Congratulations.'

'On what?'

'On the addition to the family.'

'What *family*?'

'You, Dev, me, Easy Connection.'

'No family. We're both orphans.'

'Not now, Cathy.'

She turned away. 'You're ahead of me. The addition may not be permanent.'

Alun came back with too much strong beer and everybody got rather drunk, except Cathy, who fell asleep with her head against Dev's shoulder.

She woke, next morning, in her bed, having no recollection o how she had got there.

'Dev,' said Julie, her head in her hands at the breakfast table. 'De carried you in and put you to bed. He's very strong, isn't he?'

Cathy did not answer. She thought, blushing, of her clothes neatly folded on the chair next to her bed.

'But you . . .'

'I wasn't there,' said Julie, looking away. 'I was . . . busy.' A slow, dark colour crept into her cheeks.

'Julie!' Cathy said, awed. 'Not *Chris*! But what about Ray?'

'What about him?' Julie was sullen. 'Look, Cathy, I've got a bad head this morning. I'd rather not talk, if you don't mind.'

Cathy felt cold. Did Dev and Chris sow seeds of destruction everywhere they went? Julie had been happy with Ray. She knew, without thinking about it, that Chris was not serious.

At College the next evening she turned away from her easel and found Dev sitting patiently on a stool nearby, watching her. Her heart seemed to miss a beat as it always did when she came upon him unexpectedly.

'What are you doing here?'

'I've come to collect you before you skip off somewhere.'

'How did you get in?'

'The porter knows me. I was a student here myself, remember?'

She had forgotten. She looked at him nervously. He was staring at the large paintings on the easels.

She was more than three-quarters through *Sunday Afternoon*, with Nick lying on the sofa, the pin wall and the old mirror reflecting other parts of the room. She was satisfied with the painting and because it was coming on so well, and because she felt, desperately, that time was running out for her, she had started on yet another painting, working on the two alternately, so that she did not have to wait long for drying.

The new painting was even more ambitious. Two metres high, it was incredibly complex. A kaleidoscope of shapes, veils of iridescent, glinting light, half-seen people, and the central figure, partly obscured, partly seen with supernatural intensity. She was calling it *Hampton at Azra's*.

Dev sat staring at the paintings as she cleaned her brushes and wiped the mixing area of her palette. Then he looked at the completed *September Song* against the wall, and came and looked at the two larger paintings again.

'What do you think?' For some reason his opinion was important to her. Perhaps it was because he collected de Staels. Whatever the reason she felt as nervous as when she discussed her work with her personal tutor.

'They're good. Brilliant, even.'

He looked at her, an odd expression in his eyes, almost as though he was seeing her for the first time.

'I'll have to take great care of you, Cathy, love. I don't want to look an even worse villain in the history books.'

'What history books? What are you talking about?'

He went on staring at the paintings.

'What's the matter?'

'Nothing.'

'Yes, there is.'

'All right. That's Nick lying there. I told you to forget him, but here you are painting a bloody masterpiece of him. And that's Dave Hampton, isn't it? *I* was at Azra's too, *remember*? Why aren't you painting *me*, Cathy?'

She looked at him, stunned.

'Don't look like that. I told you, I'm jealous.'

'But you can't be jealous of Dave Hampton! I don't even know him.'

'Why are you painting him then?'

'I'm not painting *him*, exactly. I'm painting the excitement, the atmosphere, the music. I made the sketches of Dave Hampton before you came that night. I wasn't there to listen to the music. I was trying out a method of drawing, like the Japanese ... Oh, you're not listening. What's the use! I was *working*, see? But I didn't do any drawing when you played, because I was listening. I didn't want to draw. How can I do a painting like this without the drawings, the studies?'

She pointed to the drawings on the walls, where they had been pinned, having been torn from the sketchbooks, and then she threw a couple of sketchbooks over to him crossly.

He leafed through them. A lot of beautifully expressive drawings of musicians, playing, singing.

'I recognize some of these guys. He's with a new group called Test Case, and that's Ed Burke.'

She shrugged. 'Probably. I don't know their names. I don't care who they are. I just had to find people who would let me stare at them for a long while. It's the only way we could think of.'

'*We?*'

She ought to have been warned. 'Nick and I. We go out every Friday and Saturday. He goes for the music and I draw. We've been going since October.'

He said nothing but went on looking through the books. There were a lot of drawings of Nick too. Nick sitting, Nick watching TV, Nick drawing. Nick lying on his side on his bed, reading.

'You're obsessed with him.'

'He knows what I'm trying to do. He let me draw him.'

'I'll bet.'

'What's that supposed to mean?'

'Are you still making love?'

She was so angry, she could not trust herself to answer. She got her jacket and her shoulder bag and walked out of the room, but at the stairs he caught up with her and gripped her shoulders.

'I asked a question.'

'Let me go.'

'*Tell me.*'

Her voice was icy with contempt. 'Listen, this is going to be difficult for you to understand. Not all girls are like the ones who go with rock stars. After you finished with me I was frightened of any man coming near me. Even in the bus queue. I felt dirty and I wanted to hide away from everybody. And then there was Nick. He helped me. Just being gentle, and interested, and loving and helpful.' She swallowed. 'We didn't need to have sex together – like, l-like ... dogs in the park. It wasn't like that with *us*. I love Nick, and he loved *me* – until you ruined it for me.'

'You're expecting me to believe ... ?'

'I don't expect you to believe anything. I don't know why I'm explaining anything to you. I don't even know why I'm talking to you. I'm amazed sometimes that I can stay in the same room with you!'

'Cathy ...'

'Take your hands away,' she said quietly. 'I swear that if you put your hands on me again without my consent, I'm going to call the cops, rock star or no rock star. Let me go, and *stay away from me*.'

She pulled out of his loosened clasp and walked stonily down the stairs. For a moment the misery in her mind acted like a laser and illuminated the whole of her situation quite clearly with its obvious solution, but emotionally she could not yet accept it, and she hurried home, trying not to think, as if the hounds of hell were at her heels.

The word had gone round the College that Chris Carter and Paul Devlin of Easy Connection were practically living at the flat in Hamilton Square, and on Saturday night anyone who had the slightest excuse or an invitation to call, turned up on the chance of seeing them. Guitars were produced by members of the College group, including Nick. Some people had brought bottles of wine. Alun was again despatched to buy beer and cider and crisps and soon one of the best of all the parties ever held in that basement flat was under way.

Cathy, coming home tired but happy from her day's painting, walked into the middle of it. Neither Chris nor Dev was there. She did not think either of them would be coming to the flat again.

In any case, it was Saturday. They would probably have a concert miles away. Suddenly she felt free and alive. Whatever happened she was going to enjoy herself tonight, because it might be the last opportunity for a very long time.

She showered hastily and changed into the long skirt and low-cut blouse with huge sleeves that Julie had made for her. It made her look like a medieval lady, she thought, happily. She brushed her long hair until it shone and went to join the dancers, with a kind of feverish gaiety. With Dev and Chris absent she felt relaxed for the first time in weeks.

It was later, much later, when, turning, she found she was dancing with Chris. Horrified, feeling trapped, she slowed and her eyes searched through the crowd.

'Over there.' She looked towards the door and saw Dev leaning against the wall, watching her. Her heart began to thump un-pleasantly.

'I didn't know you were here.'

'You were enjoying yourself too much to notice. What have you done to Dev?' His eyes were hostile.

'How do you mean?'

'He's back on the booze.'

'Oh no!' she looked apprehensively over her shoulder.

'It's all right. Not tonight. Last night he was stoned out of his mind. Worse than I've seen him since ... well, for a long time. We had to cancel a recording session.'

'Chris, can't *you* keep him away from here? He'd be all right then.'

He stared at her. 'Are you crazy? He's been fine since he started coming here and seeing you regularly. He's written four new songs which are probably the best things he's ever done.'

'You just said it was my fault he'd gone back on the vodka.'

'What happened yesterday?'

'Ask him.'

'I have. I want your story.'

'He thinks I sleep with Nick.'

'And do you?' His voice was a shade too casual. He really wanted to know.

'You too?' she said contemptuously, and turned away.

He caught her hand. 'Come and speak to him, Cathy. Make it up!'

'Make it up!' she exploded. 'You make it sound as if we've had a lovers' tiff!'

He grinned down at her, his fine eyes alight with amusement and understanding. 'Isn't it?'

She caught her breath and looked away hastily, conscious of her hand in his. Dev was not the only danger. It was easy to forget how devastating *Chris* was.

'Where's Julie?' she said, inconsequently.

'Around.' The smile was gone.

'Don't hurt her, Chris.'

'She knows what she's doing.'

Dev was talking to two girl students, who were listening with flattering interest, but when Chris and Cathy came up, he turned away immediately.

Cathy found she could not look at him, but she knew he had not taken his eyes off her. 'Cathy,' his voice was so soft she could hardly hear it. 'Cathy, I'm sorry.'

Deep colour flooded her neck and shoulders. She stared at the floor. 'I'm not with Nick any more. I never was in that way. I hardly see him now.'

She did not know why she felt compelled to say it.

They stood together, the three of them, very close in the noisy room, with the old stereo blasting away in the corner. Cathy, her mind fully open to them for the first time, did not know they were not speaking aloud.

Across the room Alun was pouring out beer at the improvised bar made from a piece of blockboard across two chairs. Bernard was lounging against the wall next to Julie. With a beer can in his hand Alun gestured across the crowd.

'Look there, friends. It's not often you see the Anwyd clear, visiting the lesser mortals.'

'The An-what?'

'The faery gods. Anwyd. Tuatha de Danaan.'

'Oh god! Celtic mythology.'

The crowd momentarily parted and the group by the door could be seen clearly. Dev and Chris had come late from a concert. Dev was wearing silver trousers, the Atlantis stone and a shirt embroidered with silver peacock feathers, and Chris had on skin tight leather trousers and a long, sleeveless black robe with signs of the zodiac glittering all over it. A thick iron chain hung down his bare chest. Fancy dress, but they wore it unselfconsciously.

Cathy stood between them in her long skirt and see-through sea-green blouse. The light gleamed on their golden hair and shadowed their eyes. There was an uncanny intensity about them. Strangely, they did not even seem to be talking, just looking at each other.

'Visitors from another galaxy,' said Julie, trying to laugh.

'Making a psi connection,' added Bernard. 'He's got her.'

'They've both got her,' said Alun. 'She won't get away now. They belong together. Look at them – beautiful they are.'

'The baby's beginning to show,' said Julie.

Alun took a deep drink from his can. 'The faery lords have stolen her away . . .'

'You're drunk, Alun,' said Julie, recovering. 'There's nothing faery about Chris, I can tell you.'

As they watched, they saw Dev put his arm round Cathy, and she turned towards him like a sleepwalker. They began to dance, very slowly, to the smoochy music someone had found.

Chris came over to them, his face closed, and drank a beer straight off. In a minute he was laughing, surrounded by three or four girls from the College, who wanted to hold his iron chain as an excuse for touching him.

Later, Dev and Chris played on borrowed guitars, and later still, when nearly all the visitors had gone, and the lights had been turned low, Chris sang the blues. His voice was harsh, sensual.

> *'I'm afraid I love you, and I've tried so hard not to.*
> *You are so young and lovely, what can a poor man do?'*

He looked directly across to where Cathy sat entranced.

> *'Now blues and trouble walk hand in hand*
> *Never had these blues until I loved my best friend's woman.*
>
> *Did you ever wake up lonesome all by yourself,*
> *And the one you love was loving someone else?'*

As it got light on Sunday morning people began to drift off. Chris disappeared with Julie, and Dev, kissing her softly, said, 'Cathy? Sweet little baby?'

He felt her uncontrollable movement away from him. He put his arms round her and pulled her close again.

'I can't. Please, I can't ...'

He held her firmly. 'All *right*, don't panic. I'm not going to hurt you. Just stay with me.'

They sat on the floor in front of the electric fire, leaning against the sofa. After a while he went to sleep with his head in her lap, and because it seemed the natural thing to do, she put her arms round him and held him.

They cleared up in a leisurely way, everyone helping, and Dev and Chris took them out to a long, hilarious meal at a Greek restaurant in Soho. The owner knew them, and in no time at all the owner's brother-in-law, a bouzouki player, had Chris, Alan and Bernard, dancing a kolo with Julie's scarf. They all drank ouzo, and the party spread to the neighbourhood, and assorted friends came to join in.

Cathy watched quietly. She was intensely aware of Dev lounging beside her, one arm round her shoulders, his fingers twined in her hair and the other exploring her hand with his long fingers. Whenever she was near him he seemed to need to touch her. She had thought that his obsession with her would have been over by now. But it seemed to be getting worse.

She felt she was in a state of emotional chaos. She was furious with herself for giving in to Dev's physical magnetism again. It was as though she was struggling in an entangling net, unable to get free.

'What does he *want*? What's he come here for?' Cathy said, desperately, to Bernard, Nick and Alun, eating late in the kitchen on Monday.

Dev had gone on to a recording session after sitting barefoot and cross-legged on her divan for most of the afternoon and evening, surrounded by pieces of paper scribbled over with music and odd marks, like a code.

'What are these?' she had said, coming in. 'Secret messages from Anarres?'

He grinned. 'A new song.'

'No, I mean these with the funny marks.'

'A new song. They're my production notes. I produce our records.'

'I thought rock musicians couldn't write music.'

He shrugged. 'Some can't. It's not necessary. Aren't you going to ask me what the song is called?' He sounded like a little boy.

'I thought Chris wrote the words.'

'Not always. Sometimes he writes the words first, sometimes I write the music and tell him what it's about, and sometimes I write the words too. I'm calling this *Cathy Sleeping*.'

She flushed and began to pull out some drawing paper.

'You may not want to paint pictures about me, Cathy, but that doesn't stop me writing songs about you. Half our new album is about you.' He looked at her sideways. 'Chris gets really turned on.'

She had stiffened, and was angry when she heard him laugh.


'They're always sitting around here. Haven't they got anything else to do?'

Bernard grinned and stretched his huge bulk. 'They've got you staked out, young Cathy. They don't trust us, and you might skip off again.'

'But Chris comes for Julie.'

'Does he?' Bernard grinned.

'I think maybe Dev's just trying to get you used to him. Prove he's just ordinary, like everybody else,' said Nick, offhand.

'*Dev? Just like everybody else?*' Her voice rose. 'Have you seen him today? He's got this long pigtail down his back, and he's wearing a diamond star on his forehead!'

They laughed at her expression.

'All the same I reckon Nick's right,' said Alun. 'Pair-bonding, that's what he's doing.'

'Pair-*what*?'

Alun leaned back in his chair, and put his fingers together lightly. 'Unlike ze ozzer animals, for ze human animal,' he began in an excellent Austrian accent, 'to mate is not enough.'

'Speak for yourself!' said Bernard.

'Vere ze long-term relationship is desired, it must be accompanied by ze making of powerful bonds of trust, giving, and knowledge. Total trust, total intimacy, equals a pair-bonding for marriage.'

Cathy said, 'He's trying to get me to *trust* him? Do you think Dev knows about this ... er ... pair-bonding?'

He shrugged. 'Your Dev is a very clever boy.'

'Not *my* Dev!'

'Oh yes,' said Alun. 'Cathy's Dev. Dev's Cathy.' He looked at her slyly. 'Chris's Cathy. Cathy's Chris. And Dev's Chris, Chris's Dev.'

'Shut up!' said Cathy, furious.


'Why are you coming here?' Cathy said, directly to Chris, who turned up on Tuesday. 'Bernard says you've got me staked out, and you come here to help Dev.'

'Maybe.'

'But why is Dev coming? He's practically living here.'

He grinned. 'He's courting.'

*'What!'*

Chris played with the salt and pepper containers. He said, slowly, 'What if I said he just wants to see you, wants to be near you?'

Her heart banged uncomfortably. 'I wouldn't believe you.'

'Well, it's true. And then, he's jealous and wants to keep an eye on you.'

*'Him,* jealous of *me?* He's really crazy.'

'He's scared you'll flit. And Cathy, you *are* living here with three good-looking guys, including your heart-throb, Nick.'

'So what!'

'So, he's got you staked out until next Monday, when you move into the flat or the farm.'

The boys had been right.

She looked at him seriously. 'I'm not marrying him on Monday or any other time. Tell him, Chris. He doesn't hear me.'

His light eyes were intense. 'Why are you fighting it, Cathy? You know it's inevitable. we all knew, that first day, when we walked across the field at Cox's Farm.'

She was very frightened. 'It's not inevitable. I don't believe in Fate.'

'Not Fate. Karma.'

He went away just before Julie came in. Cathy said, uncomfortably, 'Julie ...'

'All right, I know what you're going to say. But it's all right. I love Ray. Really I do. But, well, I've been with him since I was fifteen ... and he's away for that course. And Chris is so marvellous. He's my favourite singer ... I'm not cheating Ray.'

'Aren't you?'

'It's not anything serious,' said Julie, impatiently.

'It's all my fault for bringing them here,' Cathy said, bleakly.

# *Fifteen*

As she was finishing *Sunday Afternoon*, the next day, Tom Gibbon lounged in with a short, very thick-set man with a bushy beard and sharp, darting eyes.

'Cathy, I've brought Caleb Crow to see you. Caleb, this is Cathy Harlow. That's her work on the easel.'

The famous dark eyes flickered over her and, shivering, Cathy recalled the gossip that he was supposed to like ladies more than was good for them. They moved on to *Sunday Afternoon*, hovered briefly, like an X-ray, moved on to *Hampton at Azra's* on the other easel and came back to her again.

She did not move but looked back at him quietly. If he didn't like her work it was too bad, she could do no better. For a moment there seemed to be a glint of respect in the depths. Then he looked back at *Azra's*, slowly, carefully, reading each section of the painting.

'It's not finished,' she said. He took no notice.

'You didn't tell me she was a ravin' bloody beauty!' he said to Tom Gibbon, over his shoulder. His voice was deep, cultured, unexpected from his rough, shaggy face.

Surprised, Tom Gibbon looked her over. seeing her for the first time, she thought, laughing inwardly at his expression. Her hair was down today, not bundled up as usual. There were no paint smears on her face.

'God, I must be slipping,' he said, his eyes riveted on her face. 'I'm getting old.'

'Pity she's a woman,' said Caleb. 'A bloody nuisance. Makes things difficult. She's bloody pregnant already.'

Again, surprised, Tom Gibbon looked her over. 'That true?'

Scarlet, she nodded.

'Married?'

'No.'

'How long?'

'About three months.'

'You'll have to get rid of it,' said Caleb.

'I can't,' said Cathy.

'You'll have to. There's still time. Your career is just starting. You can't stop now. It's no good being sentimental.'

'I mean,' said Cathy, 'I haven't got enough money to have it done as a private patient, and it'll be too long to wait until the National Health . . . I put it off too long.'

'How old are you?'

'Nearly eighteen.'

'Ridiculous,' he said decisively. 'You can't have a kid hanging on at this stage. Feeding it, cleaning it, washing nappies. Trying to stop it screaming. You'll be so exhausted you won't be able to do any work. Someone should have told you before. You aren't a cow. It'll have to go.'

Cathy looked at Tom Gibbon helplessly. He grinned. 'Don't worry. Poppa knows what's best.'

Cathy was confused. Caleb sounded as though it was all decided, as though she was already one of his gallery artists, but he had hardly looked at her work yet.

'This yours too?' He was turning *September Song* to the light.

'You can't have that. I've bought it,' said Tom Gibbon.

Caleb grunted, and let it drop back against the wall.

'Damned poacher.'

'Hey, who found her?'

Caleb smiled suddenly. His beard split apart and revealed a pair of very red lips and white teeth, gleaming like a mischievous gnome.

'How much shall I pay her, Caleb? What's it worth?'

'In three years, maybe a thousand. Right now, as an unexhibited unknown, give her £300. That'll cover her expenses and leave enough to buy a nightie.'

Cathy went white. 'It's too much. It can't be worth that. I don't want charity.'

'Do you know how much he makes a year? He can afford it.' Caleb turned to the door.

'Charity, nothing,' said Tom Gibbon, grinning. 'He's going to offer you £400 when he gets rid of me. But it won't work because I'm

paying now and taking it with me. You can borrow it back for your
final exhibition.'

He pulled a tattered cheque book out of his back pocket and wrote
it out leaning on the division wall. Cathy took it, disbelievingly
while Caleb went round the room looking at the work on the easels
and, propped against the walls, blowing with disappointment and
disgust, totally ignoring the students in the room.

'Derivative,' he said, stamping to the door. 'Artschoolitis. Well
come on. What are you both waiting for?'

'W-where are we going?' asked Cathy, trailing down the stairs
after the two men.

'To your place,' said Tom, 'to look at the rest of your stuff.' He
put *September Song* carefully in the back of his van, a second-hand
ambulance, which looked as though it might break down at any
minute, and they all climbed into the front cab.


Cathy was pleased she had remembered to make the bed that
morning.

Caleb sat on it with her folder in front of him on the floor, turning
the studies rapidly, extracting those he liked. His judgement was
instantaneous and the pile grew quickly.

He stopped only once, when he saw the drawings of Nick.

'Ah, very nice.'

Tom Gibbon, sitting on the rug, flicking through her sketchbooks, looked up, grinning.

'Feel honoured, Cathy, that's the highest praise I've heard him
give. Here, Caleb, look through this.'

He took the large book, and leafed through it, grunting. With
anyone else, she thought, it might be with excitement, but she could
not imagine Caleb being excited about anything.

He went through all the work she had done without a word and
she began to lose hope. Surely he would have said something if he
was interested. She wished Tom Gibbon had not brought him and
raised her hopes.

At last he sat back and stared at her.

'You're under age, I can't deal with you. Who's your guardian?'

'I haven't got one. Do . . . do you mean you like my work?'

'Like it? You're going to make me an even richer man, and I'm going to make you very famous. I'll get out our standard agreement, so much per year and so much per painting, on condition you let me have your total output for five years. You'll have to get a solicitor to look at it for you. You'll find I'm more generous than other galleries, not because I'm a generous man, but because I want to keep my artists after I've made them. I don't want them sneaking off to other galleries. I don't deal in flash-in-the-pan fashionables. There's not one of my gallery artists who won't be as great in fifty years as today.'

'I know,' said Cathy. 'I can't believe you really want my work. I'm not ready for it.'

'I'll take these drawings with me today. I'll have my secretary send a list and a receipt. You're on the point of breakthrough, judging by those two paintings you are working on. I'll have those off you straightaway, when they're finished.' He named a sum for the two paintings and Cathy felt faint.

'I'll put some of your work in the mixed shows, and next year you'll probably be ready for a one-woman show.'

She glanced at Tom again, stunned, and he grinned back.

'What he says about being generous is true. He'll keep the paintings until your show, or put them into his store for a few years, and sell them at an enormous profit, when the time is right, and people are clamouring for your work.'

Caleb smiled, slyly. 'Don't tell her all the secrets at once. Well, I can't hang around here any longer. Are you coming?'

'No,' said Tom, casually. 'I want to talk to Cathy.'

'All right, I'll pick up a taxi. Be careful with her. Daddy may be six feet with big muscles.'

He stamped off, grinning, and Cathy went with him to the Square, helping to carry the drawings.

When she got back, Tom Gibbon was sitting on the divan looking at some gouache studies. With his long arms and legs he looked remarkably like a hunched-up spider.

'Can I get you a drink? There's tea or coffee or there might be a beer left over.' She felt shy, suddenly. Tom Gibbon was a celebrity. She had seen him being very witty and outspoken on a television chat show. Dev and Chris were even more famous, of course, but because they were not in the art line, she had not felt the same.

'Good idea. I'm parched. It's Caleb. He frightens the wits out of me.'

She looked at him and laughed. 'I didn't notice.'

'True, though. He's always three steps in front of anyone else. I can't think why I never saw you were beautiful before. I can't stop noticing now.'

Her cheeks were hot. 'I'll go and look for the beer.'

She found him surprisingly easy to talk to. He smoked, drank the beer and talked interestingly about his recent exhibition in the States and the crazy journey he had made with an ex-hippie across the country to New Mexico. He was showing her the route he had taken, in her old school atlas, his arm round her, innocently, Cathy thought, when Dev walked in.

'They said you'd left early.' His voice was icy. 'They didn't tell me you'd left with . . . a friend. I guess I'm interrupting.'

He leaned against the fireplace and looked at the room wreathed in cigarette smoke and beer fumes, their discarded coats thrown down, drawings all over the floor.

'Dev!' Tom Gibbon got up laughing. 'For Pete's sake, what are you doing here? I thought you only went round now with fifteen armed guards and police outriders.'

'Hello, Tom.' He did not sound at all cordial.

Cathy was dazed. 'You know each other?'

'Same year at the London,' said Tom. 'He was better than most of us, but he didn't work.' He laughed.

But Dev wasn't laughing. He was wary and still, poised for trouble.

'What are you doing here, Tom?'

'He brought Caleb Crow of the Arundell to see my work,' Cathy said, hastily. 'Tom's bought my *September Song* for three hundred pounds. Isn't that marvellous?'

'Where's Caleb?'

'Oh, he went, hours ago,' said Tom cheerfully. 'We've been talking.'

'I can see you made yourself at home.'

Tom got the message suddenly. 'Something the matter?'

'What are you doing in my girl's room with your arm round her?'

148

'*Your* girl?' He glanced at Cathy. 'So that's why you're not married.'

He began to laugh. 'That Caleb was right again. He said to watch out for Daddy. That he'd be six feet with big muscles. Worse. Daddy's got an ABA Certificate, a trigger temper, and a reputation for being the dirtiest fighter ever taken into Vine Street ...'

Dev half-grinned, reluctantly.

'I remember your reputation, too, Tom Gibbon, and it wasn't for fighting. I said, *what are you doing with my girl?*'

'If you feel that way about her you ought to marry her.'

'I do and I am. Monday afternoon. You can come to the wedding if you like.'

Tom looked at her, surprised. 'You didn't say.'

'It's not true,' said Cathy. 'I'm not getting married. I keep telling him.'

'Caleb won't like it. You're too young. He doesn't think domesticity suits young painters.'

'Tell Caleb to mind his own ... business,' said Dev.

'She is his business,' said Tom, grinning. 'Gallery artist under contract.'

Dev's eyes reached her. She looked away.

'Sod Caleb!'

Tom laughed. 'Still the same old Dev. You don't change.'

Dev smiled reluctantly. 'By the look of it, neither do you. I see you hit the big time.'

'Not like you. I saw one of your concerts in the States in July. Sixty thousand people, riot police, motorcade, private aeroplane, the lot, man. You and Chris have come a long way from banging out on those old guitars in the studio, and old Maurice cursing at the noise and saying it wouldn't get you anywhere.'

This time, Dev laughed outright. 'The last time I saw you was the night the police bust the Students' Union, and we got out through the skylight in the girls' lavatory.'

'There'll never be another year like us,' said Tom, winking at her.

'No, I don't suppose there will,' said Cathy, so seriously that they both laughed.

'Sorry you've got to go so soon,' said Dev, picking up Tom's jacket and handing it to him. Cathy was outraged at his rudeness, but Tom shrugged it on, laughing.

'Scared I'll make revelations to your lady?'

'She thinks the worst of me already,' said Dev.

'Get her married before Chris sees her,' Tom advised. 'We three always wanted the same girls. Chris generally won.'

'He's seen her.'

For a moment, Tom's eyebrows rose. 'And he let you walk off with her?' He laughed. 'Don't tell me. You'd already knocked her up!'

Cathy was suddenly coldly and bitterly angry. That was all it meant to these brilliant, wild young men. You reached out your hand and took what you wanted. You didn't worry about how other people felt, especially if they were girls. They were just ... objects, like a foreign car. Playthings. Not real people.

But she went to the door with Tom and thanked him. He had, after all, brought Caleb to see her.

He looked over her head to where Dev was standing, watching them. He raised his voice, his eyes alight with mischief. 'I'll see you at the College, love. We'll have a long talk!'

Annoyed again, Cathy shut the door on him and walked back into her room and waited for the explosion.

It came at once. Where had she met him? How often had they met? Why was he here after Caleb had gone? Why had she allowed him to put his arm round her? Why hadn't she told him she was getting married? Didn't she know his reputation with girls?

She answered his questions quietly, holding her temper down, except the last question which struck her as so funny, that she laughed shakily.

'*His* reputation with girls!'

It was the wrong thing. Dev was even more furious and launched into a stinging attack worthy of a seventeenth-century Scottish preacher.

She wondered, suddenly, what he would do if she went to him, put her arms round his neck and kissed him.

Instead, she turned to her desk and let the furious words flow over her. She was remembering Caleb's words about the baby. Ever since he had spoken, the words had gone on repeating in her head and she knew suddenly that her mind had been made up, the decision taken. Tom and Dev's discussion had helped. She had no need to become a rich man's toy. She was a *person*. She could be free again.

'How much of all that did you actually hear?'

'Not much. I never listen to male chauvinism. I don't think you've the right to question me, the right to object to anything I do, or even to talk to me like that. You're not even a friend.'

'Caleb Crow,' he said, suddenly, as though reading her mind. 'What else did he say?'

'He offered me a contract. He bought paintings and drawings, and he told me to get rid of the baby.'

She turned round and looked at him directly. 'I think you ought to know, Dev, I've made up my mind. I'm going to the doctor's tomorrow, to arrange an abortion. I've got the money now.'

The colour drained away from his skin, and he looked whiter than she had ever seen him.

'Just because he told ...'

'No. He made me see how impossible it would be for me to do my work and look after a baby. Put it into words.'

'Married to me, there's no problem.'

'I'm not marrying you, Dev.'

They stared at each other, fierce and unbending.

'Why not? What's the matter with me?' For the first time he had taken her seriously. 'Just because it started badly ...'

'That would be enough. But there are other things too. I'm a person, Dev. I don't like the way you and your friends discuss me, as though I was like a ... super foreign car ... handed out as a kind of prize, along with money and fame. Why *me*, Dev? You could have a baby with almost anybody. I'd make a terrible wife for a rock star. I hate publicity. All that luxury – it'd suffocate me. And I'd hate you going with other girls ... being away on tour. I'd bore you stiff. It wouldn't last three months. And then ... there's Nick ... and there's the ... s-sickness ...'

'What the hell are you talking about?'

'You know. Don't pretend you don't. When you kiss me I get sick with the taste of blood again, like that night ...'

He remembered the occasions she had pulled away from him, perspiration on her forehead. 'For God's sake, that's nothing! You'll get over it.'

'Suppose I *don't*? I won't be made to get married because you've

decided you want a baby, and will go to any lengths to get what
you want.'

'What do *you* want, Cathy? Love? Do you want me to say I love
you? Is that it?' His voice sounded odd, hoarse.

She did not notice. She tried to control her voice.

'I want some peace, Dev. Not all this ... hounding. I want to get
on with my work, that's all. I want to be free again. I want ...'

She had not meant, ever, to say it, but the anger and bitterness,
the *truth*, suddenly spilled over.

'*I just want to get this ... dirty thing out of my body.*'

He looked at her, his eyes wide open and defenceless, the hurt
showing. Then he slapped her across the mouth, hard, cutting her
lip. Blood trickled down her chin. She made no effort to wipe it away.
Her eyes filled with tears.

'All right,' she said. 'But it doesn't alter the way I feel.'

# Sixteen

The next day she telephoned for an appointment at evening surgery, so she need not miss any college work. The doctor was very blunt and to the point.

'It may mean an operation now, which is a pity. If only you had come before.'

'I didn't have the money. I thought they said there was a waiting list on National Health. I thought I would have to have it done privately.'

'In view of your age and the circumstances you would have been a priority case. You didn't need money.'

'I didn't understand.'

'It's essential in these cases to get to the doctor quickly. If only you silly girls would realize it – instead of shutting off your mind and pretending it isn't happening to you, and then it's too late.'

'It's *not* too late?'

'No. But I'll make no secret. I don't like it.'

There was silence and he tapped on the desk with his pen and looked out of the window. He was a nice man; she wasn't just another case to send on down the line.

'I suppose you aren't in touch with the father.'

She flushed. 'Yes. He wants the baby. He . . .' She swallowed, 'He wants to marry me.'

'And you don't because of how it happened?'

'Yes, and other things . . .'

He looked at her penetratingly. 'Do you like him?'

A confusion of thought boiled in her mind. 'I don't know. Sometimes. Then I remember.'

'Physically?'

Her colour glowed brilliantly. She bent her head. 'Yes. He's a rock star. He's very attractive. But sometimes when he kisses me, I remember and I'm sick.'

'You vomit?'

'Sometimes.'

There was another silence. Absently he drew interlocking triangles on his blotter. Cathy stared at them hypnotized, and leaped in her chair when he said, abruptly, 'I think you could give it a try.'

She was shaken. '*Marry* him, you mean?'

'Marry him. Have the baby. See if it works out. It's a chance, but all marriages are chancy. If he's a star he'll have money. That helps. You'll have a home.'

She smiled, crookedly. 'He's a millionaire.'

He looked at her curiously. 'Well, then . . .'

'But suppose I go on being sick. When we're married he'll expect more than kisses.'

He looked at her thoughtfully. 'It takes a long time to get over being sexually forced. It destroys trust and pride. I'm not a psychiatrist, but I believe your vomiting may be connected with *fear*, rather than sex, if that is worrying you. You say you liked him well enough before it happened. Felt sexually aroused. So it may be a question of rebuilding trust. If you could learn to trust him it may go. You want security now. When you've got it, the fear may go as well.'

'I don't trust him at all,' she said. 'I can't imagine I ever will.' She looked grey and tired.

'Give it time.'

'There isn't any left.'

He sounded tired too. 'No, that's true. All right, I'll set everything in motion, but if you change your mind, telephone me. Think it over one last time.'


She got back to her room at seven o'clock and felt so exhausted she lay down on her bed and went to sleep.

She slept deeply and dreamed hideously.

It was the worst nightmare she had ever had. She was holding a smiling, crying foetus, small, in her two hands. Then she saw that its throat had been cut and the blood was gushing out. Laughing recklessly she lifted it and let the blood run over her face and into her mouth.

She woke, screaming and whimpering, her throat choked. Dev leaned over her, shaking her, his face white.

'For God's sake, Cathy, wake up. What's the matter?'

She stared at him a moment, blindly, her mouth filled with the taste of blood. Then she got up quickly and made it to the washbasin just in time.

Dev turned on the tap and held her head, his long fingers cool and wet against her forehead. She had eaten very little and her stomach was almost empty, but she could not stop the dry retching. After a while he bathed her face, made her rinse her mouth and drink some water. Then he held her tightly while she told him her dream, and began to sob helplessly against his chest.

All the worry, pain and loneliness of the last three months, which she had pushed away into the back of her mind, came pouring out to engulf her. She could not stop crying. She had been so strong and sensible, now there was this feeble collapse.

He held her for a long time, stroking her hair, listening to her sobbing. At last he said, his voice shaking and strained, 'I'm sorry, Cathy. It's all my fault. Please don't cry any more.'

She made an effort to regain control.

'It . . . it's stupid, but I can't seem to stop.'

'Wait,' he stood up.

'Please don't leave me now. Please.' She was panicking.

'I'll be back. I'm only going to the car. Get undressed and get into bed. You're not well enough to be working tonight.'

When he came back with a leather flask, she was huddled into her warm dressing gown, but the tears were still sliding down her cheeks.

'Take this, you'll feel better.'

'I don't want any drugs . . .'

'Don't be a fool, Cathy.' His voice hardened. 'It's only brandy. I don't feed people stuff without telling them. What do you take me for?'

She drank the brandy, trying to smile. 'I'm sorry. You're looking after me very well.'

'You need someone to look after you. You're not at all the tough baby you like to think. You need someone like me, Cathy. Not Nick, wavering ineffectually around like a wet weekend.' Her eyes filled with tears again. She couldn't imagine Nick staying in the room while she was sick.

Dev filled the flask top, drank it down, filled it again and gave it back to her. 'Go on, drink up. Drown your sorrows.'

She drank again, beginning to feel warm and muzzy.

'I haven't eaten anything. I'll get drunk.'

'Julie said she'd cut some bread and butter. Cathy, I have to know ... You went to the doctor?'

'Yes. He'll recommend an abortion. But it may mean an operation now. It won't cost anything.' She did not tell him what the doctor had said about marriage and the sickness.

To her relief, Julie came in then with a plate of cheese sandwiches, and mugs of tea, and sat with them chatting while they ate, and then she went away tactfully, taking the dirty cups and plates.

Cathy felt so tired she could hardly keep her eyes open.

'Go to sleep, Cathy.'

'I'm frightened to. In case the dream comes back.'

'It won't. I'll stay here and hold your hand.'

He pulled the armchair over to the divan, pulled up another chair for his feet and settled down, holding her hand. 'Go to sleep, Cathy. I'll stay. You won't dream with me here.'

Like a child she believed him, and slept, undisturbed, deeply and dreamlessly.

When she woke next morning he had gone.

She felt rested and relaxed. She made no move to get up and go early to College, but lay thinking carefully. Think it over, the doctor had said. She must phone him today.

The dream had changed everything. She had not imagined that she would feel that terrible guilt, or that she would be so grief-stricken at the baby's death. She was not opposed to abortion as Mary was. Once, at school, she had led a discussion advocating it, and she believed deeply that it was preferable to unwanted, miserable and ill-treated babies. She felt that each woman had the right to choose for herself.

But now it had come to the point of her own choice, she found she could not go ahead. Perhaps, as a creator, she could not destroy. She would never be able to cope with dreams like the one last night.

She knew now that she was going to have the baby. Perhaps,

ven, deep down, she really wanted it. Why else had she kept putting off thinking, until it was almost too late? Yes, she would have the baby. But she need not marry Dev. He could have the child, adopt it legally, as he had suggested a long time ago.

The dream had helped to show her the other side of Dev's character. He was wild and hard and arrogant, but he could be protective and caring too. He had looked after her well last night, knowing exactly what to do for her mentally, as well as physically. He might even be a very good father.

Involuntarily, she laughed. Beautiful, elegant Dev, changing napkins, would be a sight worth seeing. Except she wouldn't be seeing it.

Was the doctor right? Was it simply the old physical fear that kept her from trusting and loving Dev? Would the fear ever go? She had trusted him last night.

She got up and dressed slowly. She had no illusions. The next months were going to be very difficult for her. She would have to ask the doctor to arrange some kind of home or hostel for her until the baby was born. She would try to arrange leave from the College. Some of her calmness went and she shivered. She would continue to work, but Caleb would probably cancel her contract now.

# *Seventeen*

When Cathy rang him, the doctor sounded pleased, and said he would make arrangements for a hostel, but she found she could not make an appointment to see the College Registrar until the following week. It was nearing the end of term now and everybody was busy.

She went up to the studio and immersed herself in *Hampton at Azra's*. She had worked so hard, it needed only another two or three days of painting to complete it. The colour was glowing vibrantly, expressing perfectly the high energy and excitement of the music and the singer. Even third-year students had wandered round to look, and sometimes she caught people looking at her out of the corners of their eyes, speculatively. She was pleased with it herself.

As it was Friday, she worked on later than usual. Dev did not appear at the College, and she thought he probably had a concert somewhere. It was odd how he never said, as though he was trying to keep this part of his life away from her.

For a moment she felt disappointed that she would not be able to tell him straightaway, but maybe Sunday or Monday.

*Monday!* Her heart jumped uncomfortably. Monday had been the day of the cancelled wedding at Nethercombe. The Vicar must have written by now.

She went home at last. On the way she bought fish and chips and a bottle of wine.

Alun, Julie, Bernard and Nick, with some of their friends, were all there in the lounge, watching television. She was surprised to see that Chris and Dev were there too, after all.

She leaned against the frame of the open door and watched over their heads, casually picking at the chips with her fingers. She felt relaxed, pleasantly tired, and enclosed in a comfortable bubble of warmth. It was nice seeing them there all together in the half-

158

darkened room. They made a brown and gold picture, television blue flickering on their faces. She stared, imprinting the picture on her mind. People in their setting. Friends. Maybe her next painting.

And then she became aware of Dev, looking at her unsmiling, his eyes blazing.

'Well, well, here she is at last, Chris. Our hardworking little baby. Here comes the bride!'

Cathy heard the tone in his voice and went quite cold. She looked quickly at Chris, who shrugged his shoulders, and went on watching television.

'I got some wine,' said Cathy. 'Anybody want a glass?'

'What are we celebrating? The murder of our son? Or the cancellation of our wedding?'

Cathy went white, and there was an uncomfortable silence in the room.

'You've heard from the Vicar?'

He got up and came over to her swiftly. Frightened, she stepped back into the hall, her hand going to her mouth. He laughed unpleasantly. 'You know what you deserve. I ought to smack you.'

The fragile trust which had been built the night before crumbled away.

He gripped her shoulders, so she could not retreat further. 'Why didn't you tell me you'd cancelled it?'

She swallowed. 'You would have fixed it up again.'

'They phoned. What kind of fool do you think I looked?'

'You don't care about that. You're mad because I outsmarted you for once.'

She jerked herself free and went on down the hall to the kitchen. He followed and sat on the kitchen table, watching as she got a plate for her fish and glasses for the wine. But she could not pour out the wine because her hands were trembling too much. When she sat down the sight of the food on the plate sickened her.

She pushed it away and put her head in her hands. She tried to breathe deeply. So the doctor was right. It was fear that made her sick.

'You really thought I would hit you just now.'

'Why not? You hit me before. And you made me have sex.'

'Cathy, why do you fight me all the time? I'm sorry. I've done my best to make up for what I did. Are you going to go on punishing me for the rest of our lives?'

'I'm not trying to punish you. I'm frightened of you.' She stared at the bottle of wine, her voice expressionless. 'I did buy the wine to celebrate. I phoned the doctor today and told him I'm going to have the baby after all. That I didn't want an abortion. Not after that dream. I couldn't do it.'

He drew in a ragged breath, and put out his hands to her, but she did not notice. 'Cathy . . .'

'I'll go into a place for unmarried mothers, and when I've had the baby, you can have it if you want. Adopt it legally.'

He said slowly, incredulously, 'You mean, you'll pass him over, just like that?'

'You want him. I think you'll see he's looked after. I couldn't keep him myself. I've got to work.'

Suddenly he started to laugh. She shrank back in her chair.

'And you, what happens to you?'

'Perhaps they'll let me continue the course afterwards . . . oh, I see what you mean. I promise I won't ask for access. I won't try to see the baby. He'll be your son entirely.'

'And you'll just fade away?'

'Fade out of your life, anyway.' She half-smiled. 'I promise I won't bother you.'

'And what about *me*? Suppose I'm not ready for the fade-out?'

'But you'll have what you want. You'll have the baby.'

*'Great!'*

She was frightened. 'What's the matter now? Why are you acting like this? I thought you'd be pleased. I thought you wanted the baby.'

'I don't think I ever heard anything more cold-blooded. You're willing to trade the baby to get rid of me, so you can go off, hand-in-hand, with darling Nick, or maybe I'm out of date and it's Tom Gibbon.'

'What are you saying?' she whispered. 'It isn't like that.'

'But get this,' his voice was venomous. 'I'm not going to trade, and I'm not going to disappear, whatever you do. You think you love Nick, but it's not true. Cathy, you could fall in love with me very easily. Why go on fighting it? You think I don't know how I affect you?'

160

She looked up at him then, her cheeks flushed, but her eyes were direct. 'Me – and half the women under thirty on both sides of the Atlantic. There's nothing different about me.'

'You felt like it at the Farm, before you even knew who I was!'

'It's just physical, Dev. You're just about the most attractive person I've ever met. You and Chris. And there's the ... magnetism. I don't know what it is, but love isn't that. It's wanting to be with someone to talk to, wanting to take care of them.' She picked at a splinter on the table. 'Trusting someone absolutely. Building a home ...'

His voice was savage, shocking her out of her daydream.

'Crap! I don't want to hear about your mooney, teenage love. You know nothing about it. Love is a rat-trap, Cathy, and you can't get out and you don't care if it kills you. It's crawling back, when your pride has been humiliated past belief.'

He was talking about the woman he had been in love with last year, who had hurt him so much. Cathy felt a sudden stab of pain.

He laughed. 'It's physical, all right. And it's hearing your woman, beautiful and glowing with your baby, say she only wants the dirty thing out of her body. It's hearing her say that you're not even a friend – *and still loving her.*'

She drew in her breath sharply, painfully.

'And that's the sort we're both going to have to settle for, Cathy. Because I'm not trading it, even for the baby. I'm not going to disappear. I'll be around permanently. And when I say around, I mean *here.*'

He walked out and she saw him go along the hall and into her room.

She was trembling and very shaken, scarcely believing she had understood him. It wasn't true. He *couldn't* be in love with her. He had never said anything. And what did he mean about being *here?*

She got up shakily, drank a glass of water and went reluctantly along to her room.

'Dev.' He was lying on her bed, his head buried in his arms, but when he turned over, there was no trace of tears, only the recklessness she hated and feared. 'I don't understand. What do you mean?'

'I don't mean sitting up in an armchair, holding your hand.'

A slow, deep colour began to rise in her cheeks.

'That's *right!*' he said, laughing, watching her face. 'You've got it in one.'

'No.'

'So, all right. You won't marry me. But you're having my baby. You're my woman, and you'll live in my house and sleep in my bed. And tonight I'll sleep in yours. I'm not leaving here without you.'

'I said, no!' She was panicking. She felt utterly powerless against him. 'You've got to go. You can't stay here. *And I'm not your woman!*'

He stretched out on his back and put his hands behind his head, smiling that glittering smile. 'How are you going to get rid of me?'

He let his eyes move over her in a way that started her heart pounding again. 'Don't fight it,' he said softly. 'I love you, Cathy. I won't hurt you.'

'No! I'm not ready. Dev, I mean it. You must go. If you don't I'll ... I'll call the police. I swear I will.'

'You're so beautiful, Cathy.'

She felt the hysteria and panic rising. If she stayed she would give way. She spun on her heel and fled into the hall, cannoning into Bernard. He gripped her arms, laughing.

'Now where's this wine we're all waiting for ... why, Cathy, sweet, what's the matter?'

'He won't go. He says he's staying all night. Oh please, Bernard, make him go. Talk to him. He won't listen to me.'

'He must be drunk.' He went in and looked at Dev, still lying relaxed on the bed.

'Cathy says you won't get out.'

'That's right.'

'Now come on, Dev. A joke's a joke, but you're taking it too far. Cathy's really upset.'

'No joke. I'm not going. Get out, Bernard. Mind your own business.'

'I share this flat. You've become an undesirable visitor.'

Dev sneered. 'You going to see me off the premises?'

'That's right!' said Bernard, joyfully, scenting a fight.

He went forward, further into the room, but Dev moved so quickly that even Cathy didn't see him hit Bernard. Bernard went down, his huge bulk knocking over the make-shift desk. The desk lamp hit the floor and the lamp exploded, fusing most of the lights in the flat, except the hall and the kitchen.

Cathy, straining her eyes in the half-light, saw that Bernard was on his feet again, briefly, before Dev knocked him down again.

'Stop it!' cried Cathy, anguished. 'Stop it! You're wrecking my room!'

Everybody in the flat was milling about in the hall, laughing, swearing, wanting to know what was happening.

'Let me *through*!' Cathy lost her temper completely. 'I want to get to the phone. I won't have them wrecking my lovely room!'

A police car with two young policemen came in ten minutes. By that time the fight was over and Bernard was lying on the floor with Julie holding a damp cloth on his head. Nick had located the fuse and the lights were on again, and Chris was having a furious row with Dev over the need to cancel an important gig because his hands were swollen from the fighting.

Even then, disaster might have been averted. Nobody wanted to make charges, not even Cathy, who had calmed down. One of the policemen pulled out his notebook to take names and addresses, and recognized Chris, then Dev.

'It's Chris Carter and Paul Devlin of Easy Connection,' he said, in a half-aside to his friend, impressed.

The second policeman looked at them, disgusted. His reply was disastrously audible. 'I can't stand these pansy hopheads.'

Cathy saw Dev's face and tried to grab his arm. But Chris laughing, said, 'My turn, Dev.' He turned, almost casually, and hit the policeman hard.

The policeman staggered back, his mouth open, a caricature of astonishment, hit his head on the door edge, and went out cold. For an awful moment, Cathy thought he was dead, then she saw, thankfully, the rise and fall of his chest. He was breathing.

The other policeman sprinted to his car to radio for reinforcements and Dev and Chris, clutching each other like drunken men, staggered about the room, hysterical with laughter, while the rest of the flat mates looked on appalled.

'Did you *see* his face!' said Chris, still laughing, trying to catch his breath. 'Shall we split?'

'He recognized us,' said Dev regretfully. 'They'll pick us up later. We might as well get it over with. He's coming round now.'

Still grinning, he turned to Cathy. She saw that the black desperation had gone. 'Cathy, love, ring Bill Hopkins and tell him to get over to – where will it be, Chris? – West Central Police Station, probably, double quick, before they can do us over.'

# Eighteen

McLeod at the night news desk of the biggest London daily newspaper was fed up. So far the evening had been slow and incredibly boring, with a multitude of small stories coming in, not exciting or interesting to pick up and make into a main news feature.

He looked gloomily at the important, but dull, story on monetary policy, which looked like being the only possible lead, and wondered how they were going to persuade the paper's five million or so readers that it was worth buying the paper. The other nationals were suffering too. There had been a lack of hard news for three days now.

He shuffled through the most recent pile of stories again. Milk lorry overturned on M1; two old ladies mugged in Ealing; a school closure owing to suspected food poisoning; Chris Carter of Easy Connection had knocked out a policeman in a fight, when the police had been called to eject Paul Devlin from a girl's flat in Hamilton Square ... This was more promising. Good for half a column, maybe, with a pic. Nothing new though. Carter and Devlin were in more punch-ups than anyone cared to count. But still he hesitated, considering. There was something at the back of his mind. His newsman's sixth sense was beginning to itch.

He took some of the unused stories off the spike. It had been earlier, something else about Devlin.

He found it at last. A phone-in story from their stringer at Bilston, about a practical joker who had arranged a wedding at Nethercombe Parish Church for Paul Devlin and Catherine Harlow. The Vicar was very annoyed.

An odd kind of joke.

He thought about it and felt a familiar stirring of excitement. Suppose it wasn't a joke? Suppose Devlin had been getting married secretly. Now that would be a really tasty headline for the millions of pop fans. But why would he be getting thrown out of a girl's flat? Could this Harlow girl live there? And where did Carter come in?

He picked up the phone and dialled. 'Don, you're the Pop Page expert. You heard any rumours of Paul Devlin getting hitched? Mmm ... Oh yes, I'd forgotten that trouble in the night club. You don't recall her name?' He looked up triumphantly at his secretary. 'Cathy Harlow or Marlow! Who is she? Where does she live? Okay, do that. Ring me back as soon as poss.'

He crashed the receiver back, and raised his voice.

'Ed? In here, quick. There's a nice little story breaking.'

Chris, bailed out by Bill Hopkins, and Dev, regretfully released with a caution, because no one at the flat would make charges, came out into the cold night air from the police station.

A man opened his car door and came across the pavement to them.

'Mr Devlin, it's about Catherine Harlow ...'

Dev spun round. 'Cathy! What's happened to her?'

The man grinned and flashed his press card. 'Just wanted to know if you knew her ...' and was saved from Dev's right hand by Bill, who grabbed Dev with unexpected force and pushed him, off-balance, into the waiting limousine.

'Are you off your nut?' His voice was like a shower of icy water. 'We're in enough trouble. That was Ed Smith of the *Mirror*. The story's out. You'd better make up your mind what you're going to say about Cathy.'

'Not to mention Cathy's baby.' Chris was laughing. 'They'll crucify you, Dev.'

Bill groaned. 'I'd forgotten that. There's no point in getting the girl away. They'll have got to her already. Will she talk?'

Dev shook his head, gloomily.

Chris went on laughing. 'Can't you just see the papers tomorrow? An innocent young girl, forsaken in her time of trouble by the wicked millionaire megastar of notorious Easy Connection ... with a nice pic of Cathy, looking like a sexy angel. You going to tell them you've been trying to get her to marry you for four months, Dev?'

'Shut up.'

'It'll be like one of the old melodramas. You'll be the lecherous villain. You'll need a black moustache.'

166

Dev began to laugh. 'I'll get a cloak. I've always fancied a cloak. And a big hat with a wide brim.'

'You're mad! Both of you,' Bill Hopkins said, angrily. 'You won't be laughing tomorrow.'

Chris said, not laughing now, his voice cold, 'Bill, if we don't laugh we might start to cry, and that wouldn't do much for our image – would it?'

They *had* got to Cathy first.

At twelve-thirty, there had been a reporter on the doorstep asking for her. Awakened abruptly and called to the door, just as she had finally drifted off to an exhausted sleep, Cathy was dazed and confused. To the reporter's satisfaction, she panicked.

'*No, I don't* know Paul Devlin!' she said, and shut the door.

Grinning delightedly, the reporter sprinted for his car. Just what he needed. A complete denial at this stage would stoke the fire nicely. Better still, unless he was losing his marbles, the girl was expecting. Who needed paraffin?

The lack of hard news continued through the night, so the scoop had a clear field.

Early next morning, on her way to College, Cathy bought a newspaper to see if there was anything about the fight, and stood in the middle of the pavement, faint with horror.

Next to a large photograph of Dev, the enormous capitals stretched down the front page: DEV'S SECRET LOVE, *Easy Connection On-off Mystery Wedding. Cathy says, 'I don't know him.'*

Was Dev getting married? Why was he evicted from Cathy's flat? Why was the secret wedding cancelled? Who was Cathy?

The *Sun* and the *Express* picked up the story in their second editions. There was a brief news item on the radio news bulletin.

The story had begun to roll.

Cathy, returning to the flat at lunchtime, found a line of cars parked illegally along the pavement. It was only when she was into the middle of the lounging group of photographers outside the flat, that she realized they were there for *her*.

'That's her!' There was a shout from one of the cars. Car doors slammed, and the photographers were galvanized into action, but they were too late. Cathy, with a speed born of terror, slid between them like an eel, with her hands covering her face and made it to the flat. Julie, who had been watching anxiously for her, opened the door and slammed it shut after her.

'Oh, Cathy! They've been here all morning. We've stopped answering the door and the telephone hasn't stopped ringing. What on earth are you going to do?'

Cathy stared at her wildly and burst into tears.

Hard news continued thin all day, and although the story was off the front page of the evenings, in favour of the football results, it was the leading story inside.

Comfortably under siege in his London flat with three security guards outside, Dev was refusing to comment. But more facts about Cathy had become known, and the story was building up nicely.

She was only seventeen. She was a brilliant student at one of London's leading art colleges, already under contract to the prestigious Arundell Gallery, and a friend of the well-known painter and TV personality, Tom Gibbon. She was clearly expecting a Happy Event.

The Sundays, faced with a choice of lead stories between Dev's secret marriage and two soldiers shot in Northern Ireland, opted, unanimously, for Dev.

The difficulty was that Cathy was proving unexpectedly elusive. She did not answer the phone, she did not go out and nobody had managed to get a photograph of her with a telephoto lens through the window. Not even a school photograph was available, although all her friends and family had been approached with offers of large sums of money.

Outside the flat, reporters and photographers kept vigil and made life a misery for those inside. There was constant hammering at the door and it was difficult for anybody in the flats to get in or out. Eventually when other residents in the block complained about the obstruction and noise, the police sent a uniformed constable and things quietened down.

Everybody in the flat had been approached individually to tell what they knew about Cathy and Dev. Sums of money were mentioned, some quite high. But there had been a council of war in the flat and they had all agreed to present a united front of 'Sorry, no comment! Sorry, no comment!' and everybody stuck to it.

On Monday, the reporters stepped up the pressure by turning their attention to the College and found less knowledgeable, but more willing, sources in fellow students, and rumours and counter-rumours began to add fuel to the flames.

Cathy had managed to get into College by borrowing a curly black wig from Julie, climbing over the mews wall at the back, and out through the side gate. She was determined to get on with her work, and her initial fear and despair had turned to a biting anger. She wouldn't tell them anything.

But her good luck could not last and, on Tuesday, one of the students was bribed to get a young freelance photographer into the studio where Cathy was working. He took his time, and got a stunning photograph. She was looking up, smiling and startled, innocent but sexy, with her sleeves rolled up and too many buttons of her shirt undone. Behind her, pinned on the wall, were a lot of male nude drawings. Everybody assumed they were of Dev.

The photograph, syndicated around the world, appeared in the *NME* with a balloon coming out of her head saying '*I jus' wanna be a sister to Dev!*' and Bernard insisted upon cutting it out and putting it on the pin board.

But the photograph had more serious repercussions than anyone realized at first. After the photographer had got into the College, the porters on the door were severely reprimanded by the College Principal, and security was stepped up to stop unauthorized entry. Unfortunately, it was a big college and it was difficult to tell who were students and who weren't, and the porters, angry and resentful, solved the problem by stopping everybody, to check.

This arbitrary action upset the students so much that there was a spontaneous demonstration, intended to be peaceful, but which ended in a fight, with the police being brought in, and three final-year students being suspended and threatened with expulsion.

Resentment boiled up quickly. All three students were popular and one was the Secretary of the Students' Union. The next day there was more trouble and fighting at the entrance, and a full-scale campaign was launched – meetings, posters, handouts – in an attempt to save the three.

This was all widely reported in the papers and linked to the Dev and Cathy stories. These had begun to crystallize around two questions: was Paul Devlin really getting married to Cathy Harlow, and who was the father of her child? Everybody who had the slightest contact with either Cathy or Dev was approached to crack the mystery, but a discreet silence prevailed, unlike other Easy Connection scandals, which had never been attended by any discretion whatsoever.

Tom Gibbon, asked if he was the father of Cathy's child, was reported as saying, *'Not this one, maybe the next.'*

This quote enraged Dev so much, that after throwing a can of beer at the wall of the recording studio where he was working, he went out to ring Tom, and yelled at him that any more attempts to grab his woman and his baby and he'd come round and murder him in an extremely unpleasant and painful way, which he described in detail. Even leaving out the swear words it would have been a spectacular performance, and it had the studio technicians on two floors, grinning and appreciative.

'Dev, *beloved*!' Tom's voice, insistent, warning, and full of unholy amusement, stopped him when he paused for breath.

'Dev, I've the London representative of *Der Spiegel* here, a girl from Dutch television and two guys from commercial radio. You want to talk to them *direct?*'

Dev put the receiver down and leaned for a moment against the wall, breathing hard. Then, suddenly, his eyes widened, his face changed and he began to laugh.

'That's *right?*'

Still laughing, he walked back into the studio.

'Listen, Bill, I've had an idea. You want some *good* publicity for the Connection for a change? I want a press conference called as soon as possible. Tomorrow. British and foreign press, magazines, radio, TV, the lot. I'm going to talk. I'm going to tie up that little bird tighter than a Christmas chicken!'

# Nineteen

In a suite at the Savoy, at a crowded and crazy press conference, with the overpowering scent of hot-house flowers, cigarette smoke and flash guns, and with the whisky flowing like water, Dev gave a brilliant performance, and the press got the story they had been waiting for.

The next day the story was back on the front page.

LONELY BOY, said the *Mirror*, with a full-page picture of Dev, looking sad and gaunt, and more romantic than ever.

IT'S MY BABY SAYS DEV, screamed the *Sun*.

Dev said he had fallen deeply in love with Cathy Harlow, and she was having his baby. He wanted to marry her, but she kept refusing. He had arranged the service at Nethercombe, but she had cancelled it. She would not marry him because she hated rock stars and their way of life.

'*But what am I to do?*' Dev had asked desperately. '*I can't break up Easy Connection. We've got a responsibility to our fans. I know she doesn't love me, but I want to look after her and the baby, and give them everything they need. Sure I'm rich, but it won't buy me my girl's love. And that's the only thing I want. I'm so lonely without her.*'

Cathy groaned angrily. 'I bet he even had a violinist playing in the background!'

Alun, reading it over her shoulder, laughed admiringly. 'A very clever boy, your Dev.'

'How *could* he? He must be crazy telling the papers all this private stuff, just as it was all beginning to die down.' Her cheeks were scarlet.

'Perhaps he doesn't want it to die down. Perhaps he wants the maximum publicity.'

Cathy stared at him. 'I don't understand.'

'He's tying you to him more firmly than ever. *Everybody* knows now who the father of your baby is, not just a few people privately. You'll have to let him have access. That means you'll have to go on seeing him for years, whether you like it or not. And that's not all. In future any man is going to think twice about butting in on that kind of relationship. Who'd want to take on a guy like Dev?'

Cathy groaned again. She hoped Alun was exaggerating, but what he said had an uncomfortable ring of truth about it. But surely, not even Dev would want his private feelings spread out for millions of people to giggle over?

But they were not giggling. Dev had not misjudged his public. A tidal wave of sympathy for Dev and Easy Connection began to spread. To her astonishment and dismay, Cathy found that people she had thought of as being her good friends had started to regard her coldly, with disapproval – people like the canteen lady at the College, who usually gave her an extra dollop of ice cream, or the College caretaker.

'You ought to listen to him, love. He really loves you, and he's so handsome. You ought to marry him. Give the baby a proper father and a good start in life.' The canteen lady spoke out forthrightly for all of them.

'Listen, missus, a bird in the hand's worth two in the bush,' said the man on the fruit stall, winking. 'Go on, give him a chance. It's cheaper than an eiderdown.'

'Get some ear plugs,' advised the caretaker, grinning. 'Never mind the music, think of the lolly. You can laugh all the way to the hearing aid centre.'

In a mysterious way, Cathy had started to become the wicked lady. A hard, cold girl, good-timing with her trendy, intellectual friends, spurning true love because she was too snobbish to like rock music.

It was a bad time. Total strangers came up to her in the street and argued with her. Letters started to arrive – sick, abusive and begging letters – which upset her so much that she stopped opening them, and burnt them in the grate each morning.

'You should be ashamed of yourself,' shouted an elderly woman from a bus queue. 'Treating that poor boy like that!'

It was surprising and horrible how many people recognized her.

'It's not *fair*!' she burst out to Julie and Nick. 'They don't know what it's about. They read a lying story in the paper and believe it all.'

'It's not really lies, is it?' said Nick.

She stared at him, momentarily speechless. 'Nick, you know what happened. You know all this stuff is not like it really is.'

'He's crazy about you,' said Nick. 'You know I think you ought to marry him too.'

But the worst was yet to come.

As a result of the newspaper reports, huge numbers of the fanatical Easy Connection fans found out Cathy's address and lay in wait at the flat and outside the College. Now she had to push her way through a hostile and ever-growing crowd each time she came out.

They were furious with her and told her so. How dare she refuse to marry their lovely Dev? They pinched her, tore her clothes, pulled her hair and spat in her face. They chased her along the road calling out, arguing, trying to persuade her.

'I can't stand it much longer,' said Cathy, shaking, on the third day. 'How long is it going on? Why can't they leave me alone? I haven't done anything to them.'

After a report in the paper that Dev was considering leaving the band and living permanently in the States, the fans stood outside the flat all day, chanting, 'Marry him, Cathy!' and throwing stones at the windows, until, late in the evening, the police moved them away. But they were back the next day.

The neighbours complained to the landlord and the landlord rang Nick and threatened them with eviction unless the situation improved.

Cathy forced her way into the flat one afternoon, nearly crying, only to overhear Alun in the kitchen.

'You'll have to ask her to go, Nick. We're sympathetic, but it can't go on like this. We can't afford to lose the flat. And how can we work? I'm not the only one who needs quiet. The telephone rings all the time ... banging at the doors ... and now all these fans ...'

There was an indistinct murmur from Nick, and then Alun's carrying voice again. 'Oh, all right. I know we're nearly at the end of term, but how long is it going to last? Will it start up again next term? Look, I like Cathy, but we can't go on like this. I haven't done a stroke of work this week.'

Cathy, feeling icy cold, waited for someone to speak again, but there was only an uncomfortable silence. She went quietly to her room and shut the door.

She was very frightened. She knew Alun was right. Her friends had been marvellous and loyal, but she could not go on disrupting their lives, dragging them into further trouble. They needed every bit of their time for their final show. But if she left here, as she ought, where could she go?

Even the College was no longer the refuge it had been. There, the fans had not been content to stay outside. They had made determined efforts to get in, and the police had been forced to double, then treble, the guard. This further angered the already angry students, who were still campaigning to stop the expulsion of the three who had been arrested earlier.

The College began to split into pro-Cathy and anti-Cathy factions, and *all* the factions, horrified at the way the police manhandled the fans outside, joined in a great anti-police battle on the steps. Several people were injured. The fans got into the building, and, failing to find Cathy, sat on the floor, singing an old Easy Connection song about corrupt policemen, *I wanna be free!* They were eventually persuaded to leave by the College Principal, but not before a great deal of damage had been done to the glass doors, windows and walls.

Cathy, who had been too tired and upset to face the fans outside the flat that day, read the newspaper report with mounting disbelief, staring angrily at the photograph accompanying it. It showed Dev and Chris, with a huge bunch of flowers, visiting one of the injured students in hospital. They were all laughing.

Julie, who had just got in, flopped down on a kitchen chair, grinning wearily. 'Thank God it's nearly Christmas!'

'I'm sorry, Julie. I feel so guilty about it all. I've asked the accommodation people to find me another place, but I've got to go on living here for a while. I heard Alun last night, Julie, I'll go as soon as I can. None of you can work in this crazy circus.'

Julie said, impulsively, 'You're such a kid and so alone. I wish you could come home for Christmas with me. But I'm going to Ray's family this year, and I don't know if . . .'

'It's all right,' Cathy smiled sadly. 'It's nice of you to think of it,

Julie, but I couldn't go anywhere in case the papers and the fans found out and ruined everybody's Christmas.'

'But you can't be all alone here,' Julie said, horrified. 'Dev will have to look after you.'

'Dev's enjoying himself. He's getting a lot of good publicity. It must be the first time in his life.' She pushed the newspaper across to Julie.

'You know,' Julie said, reflectively, looking at the picture, 'I don't think Dev will be nearly so wild when he's married to you.'

'*When!*'

'Sorry.' Julie bit her lip. 'Look, Cathy, I don't really understand. Why *don't* you? I mean, most of us would give our right hands to marry one of Easy Connection. And you don't find him exactly repulsive, do you?'

Cathy coloured and looked away. 'I'm all confused. He made me ... Well, he's violent sometimes. And he hit me. It's not just the scandals and the girls and the fights, and living all the time like this. There's that house, like a museum. Chauffeurs, limos, house-keepers, sunken baths ...' She looked at her appealingly, 'I know you'll think this is crazy, Julie, but it's against everything I believe in. It makes me sick to think that just one of those baths would have cost my mum's pay for a whole year. Fed a poor Indian family for two or three years, maybe.'

'But they earn it, Cathy. I mean, it's not just inherited.'

'My father thought that money was the most important thing. It was more important than me or my mother in the end. My mother killed herself with work, trying to keep us. *He* never sent a penny.'

'I don't think Dev cares much about money.'

'He's just got used to it. He's into power now. Julie, he would eat me alive. Gobble me up until there was nothing of the real me left, and then, most likely, when I couldn't rely on myself any more he'd leave me for some other girl.'

Julie shook her head. 'He wants something long-lasting. Chris said.'

Cathy laughed bleakly. 'Like four months. Don't you see, Julie, it's all over. I haven't seen or heard from him since the night I phoned the police.'

'You can't believe that.'

'I must have been out of my mind. If I hadn't panicked and lost my temper none of this would have happened.'

It was fear, she thought. Always, just as she was beginning to trust him, Dev had done something to break the trust.

'It's all over,' she said again. 'It was just a trick to get publicity. I don't suppose I'll ever see him again.'

Suddenly, the future looked very cold and empty.

# Twenty

Cathy could not sleep. She kept remembering Dev stretched out on her bed, his eyes smiling, his hands behind his head, 'Don't fight it. I love you, Cathy.' The words repeated in her head until she fell into a disturbed sleep and dreamed again of Cox's Farm.

She woke, sweating, and could not sleep again. She lay for a while, trying to think of a new solution to her problems, but depression closed down heavily and for the first time ever she began to feel it didn't matter what happened to her.

Everything had been too much. She felt worn out, had only just enough energy to get into College to complete her painting. At least she still had her course for a few months more.

She was so early, there was only one fan outside the College, a solitary boy on the steps, huddled under a coat. He looked as though he had been there all night.

'Cathy, can I speak to you? I know it's a liberty, but I had to come.'

She felt desperate. 'Please go away. Leave me alone!'

'You look ill.'

'You people are giving me a hard time.'

'Only because you're giving Dev a hard time. Look, all I wanted to say was, even if you don't think things can work out, why don't you take a chance? Dev gives us a lot of pleasure, and we're really grateful. Everyone knows he's had a rough deal these last few years. He wants you and needs you. You'll make him happy, even if it's for a little while.'

Because he was a stranger, and because she could not take any more, her anger and deepest fear boiled out.

'What about *me*? Nobody thinks of *me*. I'm a painter. A good one. Maybe one of the best, I don't know yet. *Suppose I don't have a chance to find out?* Suppose I married Dev and he – took me over? What about *me*?'

'All right!' his voice rose, excitedly, like hers. 'Then you quit. You walk out. You don't have to stay forever, do you?'

She stared at him. Dirty papers were blowing along the gutters in the biting wind. *You don't have to stay forever.*

She turned her back and went into the College, shaking. Silly to be so upset. She was so tired, everything was upsetting. She noticed the broken glass doors had been boarded up.

On the College notice board, pinned among the general notices, she found an envelope addressed to her. It was a brief note from the College Principal himself, asking her to call into his office at nine-thirty that morning.

The interview was quick and painful. Two weeks ago, even, she would have fought back, but today she sat stunned, unable to think.

The Principal was a short, heavy man with a brown face, sharp dark eyes and iron grey hair, cut close to his skull. He was a well-known and respected painter, and he had a reputation for irritability.

'Come in, Cathy.'

She sat down, straight-backed, in the chair he indicated next to his table.

He said, 'I don't like this interview. I'll say quite bluntly that I'm being made to act like a bloody fool by those above me, namely the College Governors. There was an emergency meeting last night after the riot.' He looked at her directly. 'They want you out, Cathy. The best painter we've had for ten years and they want you out. There's nothing I can do. They've made up their minds and you've got to go.'

'Go! B-but *why*? What have I done?' She could not believe the extent of the disaster. The worst, the very worst, had happened.

'They think, God help them, that you're injuring the good name of the College. You're unmarried and having a baby and won't marry the father. The image you are presenting of a typical art student at the London College of Art is not a good one, and they think anyone involved with a wild rock group like Easy Connection must be immoral and objectionable. That's the *official* reason.

'The real reason is that they are afraid of more student trouble, more trouble with the police and more damage to the building. They acted too quickly and stupidly, suspending the three students, and they want to save their faces. They are willing to withdraw the expulsion notices to the other three students if you go. They think that if you go, everything will calm down.

'If you don't go voluntarily, I'm to expel you, and if I refuse, they merely stop your grant.'

Cathy said, dully, 'I'm a scapegoat?'

He shrugged expressively and spread his hands.

She said desperately, 'Honestly, I haven't done anything. I haven't even been to the meetings. I've just been getting on with my work.'

'I know that. I had your personal tutor practically crying on the telephone last night.'

She sat quietly, thinking, trying to come to terms with what had happened. 'The three students can stay?'

'If you go.'

'C-could I come back when I've had the baby and all this publicity stops?'

He hesitated. 'Possibly. I don't know. We'll have to see. You can write to me in July. I'll do my best.'

He picked up a pen, and threw it down disgustedly. 'The best painter we've had for a long time. Quality, style, technique, *message*, and working harder than three students rolled into one ...' He looked at her. 'You'll go on working, of course?'

'I ... expect so.'

'The offer from Caleb Crow of the Arundell still stands. He rang me yesterday and asked me to get a message to you. He can't get through to your flat. He says the publicity has been good for sales, and he's sold all the drawings.'

She nodded. 'I'm glad I've kept the contract. I'll need the money.' She got up stiffly, like an old lady. 'I'm sorry for all this trouble. The police on the door and everything, and the damage. When do you want me to go?'

'Can you get your things together today? There'll be less trouble.'

To her surprise he came over to the door with her and shook her hand.

'It's hard swimming against the tide, Cathy. We think we're free to decide for ourselves, but it's a lie. You know that now. Society puts the screws on to make you do what it wants ... family, friends, teachers ... we're all in the conspiracy. If you don't go with the current, you get broken. It's a ruthless process. Don't do it, if there's an easier way.'

She stopped and faced him. 'I don't understand. Are you saying I should marry Dev?'

'I don't think it matters. Cathy, your work is the important thing in your life. Don't make the mistake of planning the future too much. Worrying what may happen. I'm fifty-five years old, and you can take it from me that when the future arrives, everything is different. Decide on the best solution for *today* and get on with it!'

He shook her hand again, and she went away, numbly, to clear her things. It did not take long. She carried her paintings down to the entrance hall, a few at a time, and stacked them ready for collection, with her bulging portfolio. She talked to a boy she knew who would take them to Hamilton Square in his van. Then, feeling hollow and empty, she collected her battered straw bag of paints and brushes, and looked around the studio for the last time.

Everyone was working busily, and a small group were laughing with her tutor at the far end. She supposed she ought to say goodbye to him, but she knew she would not be able to speak to anyone without breaking down.

She remembered the day she had come for her interview, and the delight when she had received the letter offering her a place. It did not seem possible that it was all over. One term instead of the glorious three years she had planned, lying in the grass at Nethercombe. A wave of bitterness and regret engulfed her like a physical pain. Yes, the future was different when it arrived.

She picked up her old basket and walked down the stairs and out of the College without looking back.

There was thin sleet blowing in the gusty wind. She saw with relief that the cold had driven the fans away from the College entrance. She wound her scarf over her ears and turned her collar up.

The fans were gone, too, from outside the flat, but she was reluctant to go inside. Reluctant to hear the telephone ringing. Too tired. Too defeated to fight any more. She turned away into the Square and sat on a bench. The Square was empty too, although the tall trees and bushes provided some shelter from the wind. She huddled further into her coat and stared blindly ahead. For the first time in her life she wished she was dead. The end of the road. Nowhere to turn. Nobody to turn to. The lowest point in her life.

'Had enough, Cathy?'

Dev's voice. For a moment relief flooded through her. She looked up quickly, and then saw his eyes – mocking, glittering with triumph, and the relief went away. He was glowing with energy and excitement.

She stared at him, understanding.

'So it's true! You did tell the papers about us on purpose. You deliberately stirred it all up just when it was dying down. I didn't believe Alun when he said so, but it's true, isn't it?'

He stood in front of her, tall, lithe, his hands deep in his strange fur jacket, grinning.

'Are you ready to give in?'

She looked away, wearily. 'Have you any idea what you did to us? It's been . . . horrible. We nearly lost the flat. What do you want? I suppose you've come to gloat.'

'Tom Gibbon phoned me. Told me they were throwing you out of the College this morning. I came to pick up the pieces. Thought you might be ready to stop fighting me. You know what I want.'

'More publicity?'

He looked at her steadily, not bothering to reply.

'You know just how to play the system, don't you, Dev?' she said bitterly. 'It traps *me*. But *you* use it for your own advantage.'

'It's called survival, Cathy.'

'For some. It's not fair. You can't choose. It's all a con.'

She stared down at her hands, saw they were shaking and pushed them under her arms to hide them. Her throat felt dry.

There was a long silence, then she heard herself saying, abruptly: 'All right. I'll come and live with you at the farm until the baby is born. If you want to adopt him then, I'll go along with that.'

'No.'

Shocked out of her misery, she stared at him. 'But at the flat, you said . . .'

'I've won, Cathy, and the terms have changed. Marriage is what I want. A *wife* and baby. I'm not settling for less.'

She drew in a long, shaky breath. 'No. No, I won't marry you.'

The silence lengthened again. He watched her, tense, his grey eyes darkening.

'Cathy, that night at Cox's farm ...'

She got up, panicking. 'I don't want to talk about ...' He caught her shoulders.

'We've got to. That's what's wrong between us. We've never talked about it. You've never let me explain.'

'I don't want to hear!' She tried to pull away, but he held her firmly.

'I'm not making excuses, I just want you to hear the truth. Because you never forget it for one minute when you're with me, do you?'

She said bitterly, 'You think it's the sort of thing you forget? You knew I was frightened. You made me stay – coldbloodedly planned to ... use ... me because you were all wound up after the tour. I was just a ... nothing. Someone who couldn't make trouble. You didn't like me even.'

'You think I took you just because I was bored and vicious with drink? You see – you are *wrong*! It wasn't like that at all. You have never understood about that night, what was happening, how I felt. Unimportant?' He laughed. 'I did a heavy deal with Chris to get you. I traded.'

She was pale. 'What are you talking about? People aren't – goods. You can't trade them.'

'Listen, you know Chris and I have always been together. You know we're more than friends, closer than brothers. It's always been like that, even at school. When girls came along, we liked the same kind of girls – usually the *same* girls. It caused a lot of trouble. We used to fight. But our friendship was more important and so, gradually, we came to an arrangement. Whoever saw the girl first, had first rights. If the girl wasn't interested, the other could take over. Sometimes we'd just hand over, if it wasn't important. Sometimes we shared. Sometimes we swopped, or traded. So that day – you were Chris's girl.

'He found you. He was watching you a long time in the water meadow before I came along. *You were Chris's girl*, right? He was the one who decided you were to stay. He was the one planning to

– use – you.' Dev laughed. 'And he made damn sure I didn't get to you before he did. Think back, Cathy.'

Pale, she was remembering. Dev smashing the glass furiously on the terrace. Chris protecting her from Dev. Not protecting *her* – guarding his property for his own use.

'But he knew how much I wanted you. So we did a deal – and he handed you over to me.'

'What did he ... trade ... me for?'

'Something very important to us both. Something I had which he had wanted for a long time. I can't tell you, it's Chris's business. It's the only bad mistake I've known him to make. I don't know why he did it.'

Cathy thought she understood. Chris knew all about girls. He had known she was too frightened to go with him. He knew he would have to let her go. Or do what Dev had done.

'I really thought you were a fan, you know, or a sensation seeker – we get a lot of them. I thought you had got in because you wanted me. There was the way you looked at me ... but by then I didn't *care* anyway. I was just crazy for you. I hadn't had a girl for months, and you were so soft and warm and sexy, and ... okay, so I'd seen you without your shirt in the meadow ... and we danced and kissed, and I held you hard against me and you couldn't stop shaking. I could feel you wanting me a lot, and your eyes said so too. You did want me then, didn't you?'

The blood burned in her cheeks. 'I was drunk!'

'A bit. So was I. But it was the sex we were high on, not the booze. It was more than sex too. I knew as soon as you walked in the room that night looking so shy and beautiful in my old shirt, that I'd fallen in love with you. So – I wished on the Atlantis stone.'

'You wished for a baby. You told me.'

'I wished for *you*.'

She was shaken. 'I don't believe you.'

'I thought, I want this girl to marry, to have my baby.' She swallowed, staring at him. 'And then you *broke the cord*, and I thought it was all right to do what I wanted. It was like we were married already. It was our wedding night.'

She drew in her breath sharply. She remembered standing in his arms, remembered how he had pulled the pins from her hair, and the strange, painful, incoherent feeling she had tried not to understand. She had felt they were married too.

'I just had to have you. When I kissed and touched you under the tree you were trembling and ready for me and I just ... lost control. I wanted you so much.'

'You didn't seem out of control. You seemed cold and deliberate, and fierce, l-like a demon. You had a face like a demon ...' She put her hand over her eyes, shaking.

'I was loving you so much, and trying not to hurt you, and then you ... started to struggle. You tried to push me away. I thought you had done it all on purpose, led me on, and I was so angry, I could have killed you.'

'So you raped me instead. You couldn't help yourself!' Her voice was sarcastic and bitter.

'I'm not making excuses. There was a split second when I knew I ought to let you go. That I had a choice. I thought, she's just another teaser, like the other one, and I ... went ahead. It was that simple.' His voice stopped, briefly. 'I never did that before. Not even when ...' He looked white.

Cathy said slowly, 'What other one?'

'That's something else we never talked about properly. But I can't, even now. There was a girl before you ...'

The rich girl he had been with for two years. The one he had loved and wanted to marry, who was so important to him. The one who had taken all his energy and creativity ... who had brought him to the point of breakdown.

'*She* used to do it all the time. She'd get me really worked up and then ... nothing. It made her laugh. She did it more and more. In the end I was half-crazy. But I always stopped – until that night. I thought you were just playing with me like that, or you'd lost your nerve at the last minute ... so I went ahead.'

'You were punishing *her*,' said Cathy, dully, hardly believing.

He shrugged. 'Maybe. But that's a kind of excuse too. I just felt you were mine. Like you were a part of myself. I didn't think it mattered at first, because afterwards we made love properly. You lay in my arms and you loved me back. And it was incredible, fantastic. I never felt like that with anyone before. It wasn't until you were sick and ran away that I realized something was wrong.

Even then, I just thought it was because it was the first time. I'd been too rough. It was later, the next day, when I found your painting, that I realized what I'd done. Cathy, if you only knew how much I've regretted ... if it hadn't been for that one split-second decision, everything would have been so different. Can't you understand?'

'Yes.'

Everything would have been different. No nightmare hounding. No baby. She would be painting at College. Holding hands with Nick at the Academy. Chance. Fate. Might-have-been. She could not bear it. She closed her eyes, gasping. If only ... *Don't think about it!* Don't think about the past! Don't think about the future ... She gasped again, fighting for breath.

He turned her face up. Her cheeks were wet.

'Marry me, Cathy love.'

She said, desperately, 'I *can't* marry you, Dev. I'm not ready for it. It would be a disaster. I know you've explained – but it doesn't matter much now. It doesn't change how I feel. I'm still frightened of you. I can still taste your blood. I still feel sick when I think of ... Suppose ...' she swallowed. 'Suppose I don't get over the sickness?'

He did not take his eyes from hers.

'Suppose I said, if you marry me now, I'll wait for the loving?'

She drew in a deep shaky breath. 'You'd do *that?*'

'For a while. I don't know how long.'

Colour climbed into her cheeks and burned deeper and deeper as she read the desire and love in his eyes.

'Cathy. Sweet little baby ...'

She began to speak quickly, unevenly. 'There are two things – two conditions.'

'No conditions. No terms. I want absolute surrender.'

'Then it's no use. I'll go to a hostel and have the baby adopted.' She was nearly crying. She turned and began to walk away.

'Wait.' He caught up with her and held her shoulders. 'Tell me.'

'It's for the baby. I – I don't know how I'll feel about him when he's born, and I've got to do my work. I want him to have a woman to look after him, someone who'll always be there, someone he can love like a real mother.'

'All right, but it's you he'll love, whatever you feel about him. What else?'

She swallowed. 'I know the farm is your home and you ...' She turned her head away and started again. 'I know there's bound to be other women and girls, but I want to ask if you'd promise not to bring them to the farm while the baby's there. While *I'm* there. It's very important to me, Dev. The most important thing. I have to feel secure.'

He drew in a deep breath and his fingers gripped her arms painfully.

'What do you take me for, Cathy? What women? I'm in love with *you*, can't you understand that? I don't want anyone else!'

She tried to pull away. 'Not yet maybe. You haven't promised.'

'Of course I promise. The farm is ours – for our family and close friends. Do you think I'm going to fill it up with dodgy boilers?'

He laughed suddenly. 'What about Chris? Can't he bring a girl? We'll never see him otherwise.'

She looked at him directly. 'I'm not bothered about Chris.'

He was laughing at her. 'You're a liar, Cathy. You like him a lot. I don't care – as long as you like me more.'

Her colour rose. 'Dev ...'

'Well, I've promised. Are you satisfied? Will you marry me now?'

'All right,' she said, tonelessly, so quietly he could scarcely hear. She was not strong enough to swim against the tide after all. The Principal was right. You got broken up. The system, other people, were too powerful.

'All right, I'll marry you. I think it's crazy and bound to fail, but everybody thinks I ought to, and you want it. I promise I'll do my best.'

She thought, I *will* try. Perhaps it would come right. If the sickness stopped. If she could do her work.

She turned to him. 'Dev, my painting ... you do understand? It's still the most important thing in my life. I can't change that. I don't have any choice.'

He smiled. 'I know. I only want to love you, Cathy. I don't want to stop you doing anything.'

'Maybe it could work. I'll try, Dev. I'll really try.'

He folded her into his arms, held her very close and kissed her eyes and mouth gently.

'Don't worry, Cathy, everything will work out. I swear I'll make you fall in love with me.'

She thought, I'll phone Caleb Crow tomorrow and confirm the contract. I'll get a stock of paints and canvas, and a big easel. Maybe I'll get a studio somewhere.

The boy's words came suddenly into her mind clearly, shockingly: *You don't have to stay forever.*

She shivered. She put her arms up around Dev's neck, stood on tiptoe, and kissed his mouth.

Across the other side of the Square, the photographer with his telephoto lens, uttered a pleased grunt and trotted to his car, the caption already forming in his head: *Happy Ever After.*

Better make that with a question mark, he thought, cynically.

*Happy Ever After?*

## DEAR SHRINK
*Helen Cresswell*

Oliver, William and Lucy Saxon had not been too keen on the idea of staying behind while their parents went off on a botany trip to the Amazon jungle. Had they known what the next few months held in store, they would have been horror-struck. For their relatively sheltered and happy life is swept away as disaster follows disaster.

## THE VILLAGE BY THE SEA
*Anita Desai*

Hari and his sister, Lila, are the eldest children of an Indian family. Their mother is ill and their father spends most of his time in a drunken stupor. Grimly, Lila and Hari struggle to hold the family together until one day, in a last-ditch attempt to break out of this poverty, Hari leaves his sisters in the silent, shadowy hut and runs off to Bombay. How he and Lila cope with the harsh realities of life in city and village is vividly described in this moving and powerful story.

## A FOREIGN AFFAIR

*John Rowe Townsend*

It doesn't seem like a promising party, but when the best-looking boy in the room seeks her out, Kate is flattered. But it comes as a blow when Rudi appears equally interested in her father, a political journalist. On hearing rumours of an impending revolution in Essenheim, Kate begins to understand Rudi's dual motive, but little dreams that she too has a vital part to play in the future of that country. A funny and fast-paced story about affairs of state and affairs of the heart!

## SWEET FRANNIE

*Susan Sallis*

Confined to a wheelchair, Fran doesn't seem to have much of a future when she goes into Thornton Hall Residential Home. But pretty soon there is eighteen-year-old Luke Hawkins to think about. After all, who better than fiercely independent Fran to help a young man who has just lost both his legs in a road accident?

## A PROPER LITTLE NOORYEFF
### Jean Ure

Jamie was a fool. A dolt. A clod. A weak-kneed, lily-livered yellow-bellied clod. Why couldn't he say no? It was all Kim's fault. She was his little sister and just crazy about ballet. If she hadn't insisted that he meet her after her classes, he'd still be playing cricket for his school instead of prancing about in a pair of tights. And what if the mob from Tenterden Road Comprehensive found out?

## THE WRITING ON THE WALL
### Lynne Reid Banks

Kev is a bad influence – or at least that's what Tracy's dad thinks – so she isn't surprised when her parents won't let her go on holiday with him alone. But Tracy is determined to have some fun before she has to settle down in a boring job like her sister. So she finds a good way of getting round her dad – at least, it seems a good way at the time ...

## THE SCARECROWS
### Robert Westall

While reluctantly spending the summer at his hated stepfather's house, Simon Wood takes refuge from family pressures in the old mill house across the field. A discarded newspaper shows that it has been empty since 1943, but somehow Simon knows that there's more to the mill than meets the eye. Someone or something is watching and waiting, but for what? When the scarecrows appear, he knows that it's only a matter of time before he is faced with a terrifying test.

## GANESH
### Malcolm J. Bosse

Born of American parents, Jeffrey has lived in India all his life, but where does he *belong*? Everyone in the Indian village calls him Ganesh. He likes the nickname and he likes the village, but there's more to belonging than liking – as he discovers when his father dies and he has to start a new life in America.